THE FORTUNES OF TEXAS

Follow the lives and loves of a complex family with a rich history and deep ties in the Lone Star State

DIGGING FOR SECRETS

A ruse brings six estranged Fortunes to Chatelaine, Texas, to supposedly have their most secret wishes granted. They're thrilled—until they discover someone is seeking vengeance for a long-ago wrong...and turning their lives upside down!

After Bea Fortune's restaurant opening is a disaster, she's humiliated when the local critic skewers her. But after entering into an uneasy truce with the writer, Devin Street, she finds herself entranced by the single dad, who just wanted to take his daughter for a special meal. And when her instant connection with Devin becomes one wild night of passion, they'll be bonded together forever—by their child!

Dear Reader,

Welcome to Chatelaine, Texas, home of the Cowgirl Cafe. If you have been here before, welcome back!

In *Expecting a Fortune*, Devin Street is a single dad, owner of the *Chatelaine Daily News* and a dog lover. Bea Fortune is a businesswoman realizing her dream to open a new restaurant featuring her mom's recipes. Their one night together opens the door to the unexpected. I'm sure we can all relate to change that happen in an instant!

But Devin and Bea decide to embrace their curiosity about what the unexpected can bring. This takes them on a journey with twists, turns and challenges. But they also discover wonderful rewards like acceptance, joy and love.

Speaking of love, I'd love to hear from you. Visit me at ninacrespo.com. Say hello and connect with me on Facebook, Instagram or sign up for my newsletter There, I share details about my books, upcoming appearances and my favorite things.

Thank you for choosing *Expecting a Fortune* as your new romance read. May this book provide an enjoyable escape that causes you to smile as you turn the pages.

Wishing you all the best,

Nina

EXPECTING A FORTUNE

Nina Crespo

Special thanks and acknowledgment are given to
Nina Crespo for her contribution to
The Fortunes of Texas: Digging for Secrets miniseries.

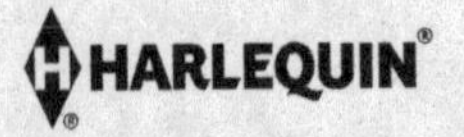

Recycling programs for this product may not exist in your area

ISBN-13: 978-1-335-59482-2

Expecting a Fortune

For questions and comments about the quality of this book, please contact us at CustomerService@Harlequin.com.

Harlequin Enterprises ULC
22 Adelaide St. West, 41st Floor
Toronto, Ontario M5H 4E3, Canada
www.Harlequin.com

Printed in U.S.A.

Nina Crespo lives in Florida, where she indulges in her favorite passions—the beach, a good glass of wine, date night with her own real-life hero and dancing. Her lifelong addiction to romance began in her teens while on a "borrowing spree" in her older sister's bedroom, where she discovered her first romance novel. Let Nina's sensual contemporary stories feed your own addiction to love, romance and happily-ever-after. Visit her at ninacrespo.com.

Books by Nina Crespo

Harlequin Special Edition

The Fortunes of Texas: Digging for Secrets

Expecting a Fortune

Small Town Secrets

A Chef's Kiss
The Designer's Secret
A Second Take at Love

Tillbridge Stables

The Cowboy's Claim
Her Sweet Temptation
The Cowgirl's Surprise Match

The Fortunes of Texas: Hitting the Jackpot

Fortune's Dream House

The Fortunes of Texas: The Hotel Fortune

An Officer and a Fortune

Visit the Author Profile page
at Harlequin.com for more titles.

Chapter One

The beautiful spring day mirrored Bea Fortune's mood as she hurried down the sidewalk. She wanted to shout out in glee to the residents of the small sleepy town of Chatelaine, *Tonight's the night!* Her long-held dream of opening a restaurant, the Cowgirl Café, was just hours away.

On some level, she still couldn't believe it was happening. Over the past few years, she'd shadowed chefs and restaurant proprietors as well as completed a degree in restaurant management. But financially, the goal had remained out of reach until her life had changed overnight.

A few months ago, she'd been summoned to Texas with her sister, Esme, and their brother, Asa. Their deceased uncle, Elias Fortune, had left an inheritance in his will for them and his grandchildren. Elias's widow, Freya Fortune, had explained how he'd wanted to make each of their wishes come true.

Bea didn't consider herself a small-town girl, but something about Chatelaine had felt right, and she'd stayed to launch a restaurant there using the windfall she'd received. Now she could finally share her take on down-home family food inspired by her mom's recipes. Fried green tomatoes on a bed of fresh basil with remoulade. Bourbon-glazed pork chops and sautéed kale. Gulf shrimp and green chili–cheddar grits, and baskets of buttery homemade biscuits served at every table. Those selections were just some of her favorites on the menu.

Growing up, the food her mother, Andrea, had prepared had been made with love. Even now in her thirties, Bea still remembered the warmth and goodness filling the kitchen as her mom had cooked—and playfully admonished Lars, Bea's dad, when he'd come in and sneak a taste from a pot warming on the stove.

More than anything, she wanted her customers to leave with that same sense of contentment after enjoying a meal at her establishment. And for the café to be something her parents would have been proud of had they still been alive.

Anxious to get to the restaurant, Bea picked up the pace. An afternoon breeze ruffled her long auburn hair. As she smoothed strands from her forehead, she spotted Devin Street, the owner of the *Chatelaine Daily News*, walking toward her. Bea's heart did a little flip-flop in her chest.

Dressed in dark boots, black jeans, and a light blue button-down shirt, he fit in with the rest of the casually dressed pedestrians. But his height—and the way he wore a cowboy hat—put him head and broad shoulders above the rest. The tan Stetson was pulled low over his deep sepia eyes, and his gaze reflected keen observation along with a confident, relaxed nature not every guy their age possessed. Add in the dark beard that was a hint more of a shadow on his angular, brown jawline, and he was worth-a-second-look sexy.

And she'd given in to the temptation to look more than a few times since her future brother-in-law, Ryder Hayes, had introduced them after she'd moved to town.

He gave a nod and a smile. "Hello, Bea."

His voice, rich and smooth, flowed like the warm golden-brown honey served with biscuits at the café.

Slightly breathless, she pushed out the words "Hi, Devin." *Jeez.* She sounded like she had a case of laryngitis.

"Ready for tonight?"

"Absolutely." Her tone rose an octave higher than normal. "Everything is great." And now she sounded like a cheerleader at a pep rally. Thankfully, Devin didn't seem to notice.

As he strode past, a wonderful masculine scent with notes of cedar, citrus, and musk followed him. Unable to resist, she glanced over her shoulder. The pair of Levi's he had on suited him well.

Before she looked away, Devin glanced back and met her gaze.

Oops...busted. On a reflex, she waved at him.

With a slightly questioning expression, he waved back.

No, that wasn't awkward at all... As Bea faced forward, the heat creeping into her cheeks turned into a blazing fire, making her feel overly warm in the outfit she'd chosen for the restaurant's opening. The lightweight peach sweater, white blouse, jeans, and flats gave her a professional look, but the ensemble also allowed her to move around quickly during dinner service.

Instead of drooling over Devin, she should have asked him if the freelance food critic was coming to dinner tonight.

The anonymous person wrote a column for the paper and rated establishments in Chatelaine and the surrounding area. Rumors swirled over where the columnist was from. Corpus Christi? Austin? Maybe Houston? But even if she had asked Devin if the person was showing up, he wouldn't have told her. He and his staff were tight-lipped about the critic's plans along with his or her identity.

Whoever it was had recently given a glowing review to the new menu at the Saddle & Spur Roadhouse, a local casual restaurant known for their desserts and the option of steak as a side dish. If all went as expected, there was a good chance they would see her restaurant in the same light.

Nervousness expanded in her chest, and she released it in a long exhale. Everyone was prepared for the midweek opening night, thanks in part to her younger sister, Esme, who was also acting kitchen manager, and Freya, who was filling in as the temporary waitstaff supervisor. The older woman had been a big help, stepping in to fill the void after the person Bea had hired for the job had suddenly bailed out.

They and the staff had worked hard yesterday preparing for the big night. And if the soft opening for the café the week prior with just friends and family was any indication, success was on their side. Everyone had raved over the food.

A few steps later, Bea reached the blue-doored entrance to the corner restaurant and went inside.

The space with light gray walls and white trim was modern, but the tan brick fireplace, Western-inspired metal wall art, and vases of brightly colored wildflowers on each table gave the place a type of intimacy that invited people to relax and savor their meals.

As she locked the door behind her, Bea's gaze landed on the nonfunctioning alarm-system panel. It was the last major task that needed to be completed in the building.

The security company was doing the installation tomorrow. An appointment with them had been set up by Esme for last week, but the company had claimed someone had called and canceled it.

A smudge that needed to be wiped away from one of the windows near the panel suddenly caught her eye. As did a basket of rolled silverware. Instead of sitting on a table, it should have been under the host stand. They were small details, but ignoring them today would just make it easier to let go of the high standards that would set the Cowgirl Café apart from other places. She would mention the issues to Freya.

As she ran through a mental list of other items she wanted to review before they opened, Bea flipped the light switch.

None of the overhead lights came on.

That was odd. Had a power surge happened again in the dining area? That situation had occurred the day after the rewiring of the building, shutting down part of the circuit panel, but the problem was supposedly fixed. Bringing the electrical system up to code in the older structure had been a major expense along with the plumbing.

On the way to the circuit panel in the kitchen, her phone rang. It was Esme.

"Hello."

"Hey." Her sister's happy mood reflected in her voice. "I'm running a few minutes behind. Sorry. But Tanya and the staff are good to go on food prep. They just have to set up the stations."

Esme's wedding day was in just a few days, and Bea was amazed at how calmly her sister was juggling planning the big day and working at the café, along with motherhood.

Esme and Ryder each had baby boys the same age, Chase and Noah, and their children were the reason they'd met a few months ago.

On the day the boys had been born, the staff in Labor and Delivery at the county hospital had accidently mixed up their identification bracelets. No one had realized the switch had occurred until Esme had taken an ancestry test.

The news had been a shock to everyone, but as Esme and Ryder had tried to find the best way forward, another truth had been abundantly clear: they were meant for each other. And since they'd become engaged, they'd been inseparable.

Bea had tried to convince Esme to at least take time off before the wedding, but she'd refused, not wanting to miss the grand opening. Admittedly, it was a comfort to have Esme and Tanya watching over the kitchen. Tanya was not only a talented sous chef, but she was good with the staff and highly organized like Esme. The two women made a good team.

"I'm sure everything will be fine, but hmm, let me take a wild guess," Bea playfully replied. "Does Ryder have anything to do with you being late?"

"Only because we were discussing the wedding and getting in some much-needed cuddle time with Chase and Noah."

"*Just* cuddle time with Chase and Noah, and nothing else? Now why do I find that hard to believe?" Bea chuckled. She flipped the light switch in the kitchen, but again, none of the overhead lights illuminated. "Are you kidding me? What's going on?"

"With me and Ryder? Honest—nothing else happened." Esme laughed. "Not that we weren't tempted."

"No, not that. The electricity is out."

"Maybe something tripped the main switch."

"I'm checking it now." Bea went to the utility closet in the hallway just off the kitchen. Inside of it, she examined the circuit panel on the side wall. "It looks like something did trip the main switch. But why didn't the generator kick in to compensate?"

"Good question. I'll add making an appointment for an inspection of the generator to my to-do list. You have enough to worry about. Just stay focused on having a successful grand opening."

Esme was right. She was letting worry mix up her priorities. What would she do without her sister and Freya to keep her straight? Bea flipped the main switch on the panel.

"Is everything good?" Esme asked.

Bea stared into the darkened kitchen. "No." She turned other switches off and on in the circuit box as well, but nothing happened. Dread started to sprout. "I've got to figure out what's going on now. We can't do anything without power!"

"Do you want me to call the electrician?"

"No, I'll do it, but maybe I've missed something." Bea walked out of the closet. "I'm going to take a look at the generator."

"Okay," Esme said. "I'll step on it. I should be there soon."

"No. I don't want you speeding to get here. Just drive safely."

Minutes later, Bea had triple-checked everything to do with the circuit panel, the generator, and searched online for outages in the area. Finally, she called the electrician and explained the problem.

"We're still finishing a job just outside of town," the woman said. "It'll be at least a couple of hours before we can get there."

Doing her best to stay in crisis-management mode versus heading straight into panic, Bea paced the dining room. "Is there any way you could get here sooner? Tonight's the grand opening of my restaurant."

"Well, I could send my apprentice. He might be able to spot the problem."

"I'd appreciate that. Thank you." At this point, Bea would take any help she could get.

As she hung up, urgent knocks sounded on the back door, which was also the staff entrance.

Bea used the flashlight on her phone to light her way past her office to the door at the end of the hall.

Before she got there, something crunched under her shoe.

A piece of shrimp? How had that gotten here? As Bea shone the light around, she spotted more of them smashed on the floor along with leaves of romaine and what looked to be some kind of sauce.

Yesterday, she'd gone out the front entrance, but surely someone who'd exited through the back must have noticed the mess. Why hadn't anyone stopped to clean it up? Disappointment pushed out a sigh. But right now spilled food was the least of her worries.

Bea opened the door.

Freya stood outside. The tall, eighty-something woman with a stylish ash-blond bob had a pep in her step as she walked in.

The waitstaff's signature uniform was a black, checkered button-down shirt, black jeans, tennis shoes, and a camel-colored bistro apron, but her fashion-forward great-aunt had upscaled the look. She had on a pair of black kitten-heeled slides, slim-legged black slacks, and she'd added an artfully knotted beige silk scarf around her neck.

"You must have a lot on your mind," Freya said cheerfully. "You forgot to unlock the door." As she peered at Bea's face her expression shifted to concern. "You look upset, honey. Has something happened?"

"The electricity is out, and the generator isn't working. I've called the electrician, but they won't be here for a while." Admitting the situation aloud made Bea a tad nauseous.

"Oh, that's terrible!" Empathy filled Freya's emerald-green eyes as she patted Bea's arm. "And everything was going so well with the plan for tonight's opening. What can I do to help?"

"Would you mind making a sign instructing the staff to use the main entrance? It's too dark for them to come in this way. And then if you could monitor the front and let the staff in as they arrive. Ask them to take a seat in the back of the dining room. I'll be out soon to give everyone an update."

"Of course."

Bea retrieved paper from the printer in her office along with a marker and a flashlight. She gave them to Freya, and the older woman hurried off.

As she sat down at her desk, looking for a second flashlight in the drawer, her heart rate amped up as her aunt's words kept echoing in her mind.

Everything was going so well...

The alarm system not being installed. Now the power

was out. Bea normally wasn't superstitious, but what was that saying about bad luck happening in threes? She had broken one of her favorite coffee mugs that morning. Did that count? *Stop.* This wasn't about bad luck. The electricity issue was just an opening-night hiccup that needed to be handled…quickly.

On the positive side, the food would remain at a safe temperature in the walk-ins and prep refrigerators, as long as they didn't open them while the electricity was out. They just needed enough time to cook the food and be ready to serve customers once the café opened.

Later on, as the electrician's apprentice worked on the problem, Bea addressed the staff: "We'll have less time to get ready, but the good news is we've already had the soft opening and we know what we're doing."

Taking a pause, she glanced around the room and met Tanya's gaze. The anxiety Bea felt was written on the young Black woman's face. This was her sous chef's first time helping to open a restaurant. She was probably nervous about that already, and this situation was making it worse. Maybe others in the group felt the same way. And honestly, could she really blame them?

Bea's own anxiety started to rise.

She looked into Esme's green eyes. Her dark-haired sister gave her a nod and an encouraging smile.

As the boss, she had to remain just as confident as Esme. Bea paused a few seconds longer, searching for the right words to assure Tanya and the rest of the staff. "I have faith in all of you. You've worked hard to make this day possible, and I'm grateful for all you've done. Once the issue is fixed, I know we'll pull together and make tonight's launch amazing!"

As if on cue, the lights came on.

Relief rushed through Bea as everyone cheered.

Esme gave her a hug. "See? Everything is all good. Don't worry—we'll be ready."

But they were opening in less than three hours. Would they make it? "We should check on how many early reservations we have."

Just as Bea and Esme started walking to the host stand, Tanya hurried toward them.

"We have a huge problem," she whispered. "I can't find any of the food we prepped for tonight."

"What?" Bea and Esme both asked at the same time.

"It has to be there," Esme said as they hastened to the kitchen. "Maybe one of the cooks moved things around?"

"I asked." Tanya replied nervously. "But they said they didn't."

Inside the kitchen, the three of them along with the cooks searched the walk-ins, looked in storage rooms, and frantically rechecked every shelf. Even if they could thaw out what remained, there wasn't enough of anything to serve a restaurant full of hungry customers.

Freya came into the kitchen. "I can hear you all the way in the dining room. What's all the commotion about?"

"The food is gone." As the truth became clear, Bea's stomach sunk to basement level. "We have to cancel the grand opening."

Chapter Two

Devin Street quickly locked up the downtown office of the *Chatelaine Daily News*. He had a very important date. He was meeting his daughter, Carly, at the Cowgirl Café for dinner.

Most nights during the week, he worked late and ate his meals at his desk. As the owner, main reporter, and editor for the paper, his schedule was full. He *did* have to do a little work on the side tonight—it couldn't be helped. He was the anonymous restaurant critic, but spending quality time with Carly was his main focus.

It had taken a lot to convince her to join him instead of going to a friend's house to eat pizza. A chance to be one of the first in her friends group to check out the new spot in town had swayed her decision.

Lately, so many things had become a struggle with his thirteen-year-old daughter. He and his ex, Lauren, were co-parenting Carly through her seemingly endless mood swings. Last year, when she'd "officially" become a teen, almost overnight her communication style had shifted from intelligible words to huffs, eye rolls, and constant groaning over the rules they laid down to keep her safe and prepare her for adulthood.

What was that saying about how your teenager's actions were payback for giving your own parents hell when you'd been growing up? Devin sighed. But had he really been *that* challenging when he'd been her age?

A vision of his father sitting behind the desk in the office he'd just left made Devin smile. Carl Street, who Carly had been named after, was probably looking down, laughing at him right then.

Carl had raised him as a single father after his wife had passed away when Devin had been just five years old. His dad had possessed the right balance of healthy skepticism, optimism, and a balanced view of the world. They were important qualities to have as a parent, journalist, and a boss. And now that he was following in his father's footsteps, he made it a priority to emulate him.

As Devin walked to the restaurant, he reviewed a text from the pet shelter asking him if he had time to foster a dog. The pet's elderly owner was moving into a senior-living apartment building and wouldn't be able to take his beloved companion with him. The shelter was trying to find the dog a permanent home before the move. If they couldn't, they would need Devin's help. Without a second thought, he responded yes.

For many years, his father had also assisted the shelter. Carl had used the experience to teach him responsibility and the importance of helping others when they needed support. Hopefully Carly was learning the same thing from him as he continued that tradition as well as giving the shelter free space in the newspaper to feature animals up for adoption.

She'd done a great job helping him take care of Chumley, a Great Dane he'd fostered last month. He'd even considered adopting him for her. But a couple who'd been searching for that specific breed had reached out to the shelter about the dog, and from the way Chumley had immediately bonded with them, it had been clear where he belonged.

As Devin finished answering messages, his phone chimed with a familiar ringtone. It was his ex.

On a reflex, he checked the time on the screen before answering. *Shoot.* He was running a little late.

"Hey, Lauren. I'm a minute or so from the restaurant. Just drop Carly out front and tell her to wait for me."

"Oh, I guess you missed the big news."

The hint of light sarcasm in his former wife's voice made him pause. "What happened?"

"The Cowgirl Café is postponing their grand opening."

"Since when? They've been advertising it in the paper for weeks."

"Since not too long ago. I suspect that no one saw this coming considering the amount of people they're turning away."

He quirked a brow. "Did they say why?"

"I have no idea, but why the restaurant isn't opening is the least of your worries."

Carly... Her having bragging rights for being the first of her friends to eat at the new hotspot was no longer a possibility.

He started walking again, picking up the pace. "I know she's probably bummed. But let her know we can go anywhere she wants tonight."

"Oh, no—I've already gotten my dose of attitude for the day. One of her teachers called this afternoon. Your daughter's been goofing off in class. I told Carly if she doesn't get her behavior in order and bring her grade back up, I'm changing her curfew to six on a school night *and* the weekends to make sure she studies." Frustration tinged Lauren's tone. "Now her hate-my-mom hormones are on full blast and I'm on the verge of losing my patience with her."

Your daughter? Devin quietly huffed a chuckle. It was interesting how Carly became all his when she was acting up. But having been in Lauren's shoes when it came to *their* daughter, he understood the exasperation she felt. "I'll be there in a sec to handle things."

A moment later, he arrived at the café.

More than a few disappointed people mingled near the entrance where Freya Fortune stood with one of the hosts.

"I'm so sorry," the older woman said to everyone. "Something unexpected has happened, and we don't have any food to serve you tonight. But we can put your name and number on our email list. We'll contact you when we have an update."

Some folks added their information to the list while others walked away, frustrated over their ruined dinner plans.

No food—that was why the opening had been canceled?

Resisting the urge to find out more, Devin jogged to Lauren's tan SUV parked farther down the street.

As he got closer, his dark-haired ex-wife met his gaze through the windshield. He went to the driver's side, and she opened the window.

Carly sat beside her in the front passenger seat, head down, texting on her phone. Their daughter had inherited his brown eyes and the color of Lauren's deep chestnut-brown hair as well as her light brown complexion.

After exchanging a look of acknowledgment with his ex, he spoke to Carly. "Well, little lady, it looks like we have to hang out somewhere else tonight."

"I guess," Carly mumbled. As she stared at her phone, her face lit up. "But Michaela said I can still come to her house and make pizza. Her dad just built a pizza oven in their backyard."

"But what about our father-daughter date? You're not standing me up, are you? We can order pizza from your favorite place and watch a movie or go to the Saddle and Spur Roadhouse for some burgers and those triple-fudge brownies you like."

"*Father-daughter* date? Seriously, Dad, I'm not ten years old."

No, she wasn't. At that age, she'd always been eager to spend time with him.

As if reading his mind, Lauren gave him an empathetic look before turning her attention to Carly. "You can hang out with Michaela and make pizza at her house another time. Your dad cleared his schedule for you."

"But I told everyone I would be eating at the Cowgirl Café." World-ending unhappiness filled Carly's face as she slumped in the seat. "Just ordering pizza or going to the Saddle and Spur is embarrassing."

Embarrassing? A small pang of sadness hit Devin, but he forced a smile. "I know eating at the Saddle and Spur isn't as exciting as trying out a new place, but..."

"So I can go to Michaela's?" Carly's expression was hopeful as she looked between Devin and Lauren.

The last thing he wanted to do was force his daughter to spend time with him. And Lauren could probably use a couple of hours to herself. Figuring that accepting a compromise was the best solution, he gave his ex-wife a nod. "That's okay with me if you're good with it."

"All right, then." Lauren sighed. "You can go to Michaela's. But you owe your dad a thank-you hug before we go."

Smiling, Carly bounded out the SUV. She threw her arms around his neck. "Thanks, Dad. I love you."

He hugged her back. The love swelling inside his chest almost choked him up. "Love you, too. Have a good time."

He waved goodbye as Lauren and Carly drove away. Standing alone on the sidewalk, he stared at the front of the Cowgirl Café and the surrounding area. It was like a ghost town. A sense of desolation set in as he walked back to his car parked near the office.

The feeling was still there as he microwaved last night's leftover enchiladas in the kitchen at his house on the outskirts of Chatelaine.

The ranch-style home had all the necessities. In the living room, a beige couch, side chairs, a solid-wood coffee table, and a media console underneath a wall-mounted widescreen television partially filled the space. The dining room with a window overlooking a small deck in the backyard was empty. A king-sized bed and dresser furnished his main bedroom, and he'd converted one of the guest bedrooms into an office.

The second guest bedroom was Carly's.

In the kitchen, one of her purple hair ties sat on the counter. Not feeling up to the effort of walking down the hall and putting it in the bathroom, he stuck it in a junk drawer. It also contained a half-empty bottle of glitter nail polish, lip balm that was also close to done, and other odds and ends his daughter had left in his truck or around the house.

He'd learned a long time ago not to get rid of anything she owned, no matter how long it sat unused or how empty it looked to him. Because as soon as he did, she would come searching for it, claiming the item was something she couldn't live without.

As he shut the drawer, he released a deep sigh. He'd really been looking forward to watching her eyes light up as they tried out several items on the menu. Her guard always came down when she was truly enjoying herself, and in those moments, he saw his little girl again.

Seriously, Dad, I'm not ten years old...

But wasn't it just yesterday that Carly had been a toddler crawling on the rug between him and Lauren in the living room of their tiny apartment in Dallas?

As Devin stood at the kitchen counter eating dinner, nostalgic memories flooded his mind.

Back then, he'd been employed at a newspaper as an entry-level reporter and Lauren had worked at a clothing store. Money had been tight, but they'd made enough to pay the bills and take good care of Carly.

Within a few years, their priorities had shifted as promotions at their jobs had opened up a better life for them. But a house and all the possessions in the world couldn't mask the obvious. He and Lauren had been growing apart. Busier schedules. Different interests. It had been a combination of a lot of things. Their love for Carly had become their main bond.

Wanting to give their marriage a second chance, they'd moved back to his hometown of Chatelaine seven years ago, and he'd started working with his dad at the paper.

But even with more balanced schedules, he and Lauren had still struggled to find their way back to each other.

Just as they'd been considering a trial separation, his dad had gotten sick. He and Lauren had rallied together to take care of Carl.

Managing the paper in his father's absence had given Devin a good look at the financials. The *Chatelaine Daily News* had been barely breaking even. But it was the one thing that had kept Carl going through the harsh chemotherapy treatments.

The image of his father, frail yet trying to remain upbeat for everyone until the end, came into Devin's mind. Lauren had been a huge help as he'd coped with the loss. But a year later, they'd been more like strangers than husband and wife. The ending of their marriage had been an amicable decision, and they'd worked out the details of their divorce with a mediator instead of attorneys.

They'd also both agreed to remain in Chatelaine. Lauren had gone back to school at the local community college, and he'd kept the newspaper. Making it profitable again had required him to whittle the staff. He, along with the managing editor, Charles, who also contributed articles, and their staff assistant, Quinn, produced the newspaper that went out online every Thursday and in print on Sundays.

When the budget allowed, he used freelance journalists and photographers to fill the gaps.

They'd been saving space in tomorrow's online edition for his review of the Cowgirl Café. But he wasn't sure what he wanted to write yet.

Done with dinner, he went to his home office and reviewed his emails and messages.

A woman named Morgana was interested in looking through the newspaper's archives. Everything from the past ten years could be accessed from their website. Anything beyond that Quinn was working on organizing and uploading to their cloud-storage account. But whatever this woman was looking for they could provide in one form or another.

After answering Morgana's email, he went to the paper's online social media page, the *Chatelaine Daily News* Community Corner. As the moderator, he reviewed the remarks from residents on posts regarding happenings in the town or teasing upcoming stories in the paper.

Usually there were just a few praises, concerns, or opinions, but the multiple comments under the post about the Cowgirl Café's grand opening snagged his attention.

New restaurant in town is a huge disappointment...

The Cowgirl Café ruined my sister's birthday...

New restaurant owner needs a lesson on customer service...

No food? Way to screw up opening night...

The chatter was brutal...but honest.

Devin pulled up the Cowgirl Café's website. A statement was on the welcome page.

Due to an unforeseeable incident, the Cowgirl Café's grand opening has been postponed. We apologize for the inconvenience and hope you will join us when we reschedule this celebration...

Freya Fortune had said they didn't have food to serve customers. But when he'd asked Bea earlier that afternoon if she was ready for the grand opening, she'd given him an enthusiastic confirmation. What type of unforeseeable incident could have caused a cancellation? Incompetence? Poor planning?

He worried his lower lip, mulling it over. Bea's response didn't fit with either of those scenarios. But the statement the Cowgirl Café had issued wasn't disputing Freya's explanation. And as a restaurant critic, it was his job to give an unbiased opinion.

But he didn't want to make Bea look bad either.

The memory of Bea walking past him on the sidewalk flashed into his mind. Along with the tingling sensation along the back of his neck that had made him look over his shoulder.

He'd been surprised and pleased to see her glancing back at him. Had he really glimpsed a sparkle of interest in her eyes? Or had he imagined what he'd wanted to see? That if he could ask her out, there was a chance she would say yes.

As he let the wonderful daydream of that moment run through his mind, a slight smile tugged at his mouth.

Another comment appearing under the social media post for the Cowgirl Café pulled him back to the present.

Having food on opening night is Restaurant 101 in the industry. Maybe the owner needs to find a different hobby to occupy her newfound wealth and time...

Devin sat back in the chair. That was harsh. But was the commenter right?

Chapter Three

Weariness weighed on Bea as she trudged down the carpeted steps of her two-story condo dressed in a faded blue sleep shirt. When she'd awakened, she'd hoped last night's canceled grand opening of the café had just been a bad dream. Unfortunately, it was a nightmare that had actually happened.

After the successful soft opening, she'd felt exhausted but elated and ready to conquer the world. She'd anticipated experiencing the same high with the café's official launch last night. Not this sense of failure, embarrassment, and utter confusion.

Of all the things that could have happened with the grand opening, the last thing she'd expected was for someone to steal the food. They'd broken in through the back office. Everyone had been so focused on the problem with the electricity they hadn't noticed the shattered window until after they'd realized the food was missing.

The police had asked if there was someone Bea was aware of who might have a grudge against her or the restaurant. Maybe a current staff member or an applicant she hadn't hired had decided to get even about something? But she couldn't think of anyone. Even the managers of the other restaurants in the area had wished her well. And all the workers seemed genuinely upset over the turn of events.

Just as she reached the bottom step heading for the kitchen, the doorbell rang. She took a detour in the opposite direction and answered the door.

It was Esme. Dressed in jeans, an oversized navy sweater, and heels, she looked a little tired but more refreshed than Bea.

On the way in, she gave Bea a tight hug. "You don't look like you got much sleep. Are you okay?"

Bea hugged her back. "I think I'm still in shock."

"I am, too." Esme followed her through the adjoining archway.

In the kitchen, professional-grade stainless-steel appliances and dark granite counters were balanced with whitewashed wood cabinets and lots of natural light from the bay window in the breakfast nook.

Herbs thriving in pots on the windowsill and a bowl of fresh fruit on the table gave the space a homey appeal.

"Coffee?" Bea set up the Keurig on the counter with water and grabbed two coffee pods.

"Please." Her sister took two mugs from an upper cabinet and handed them to her. "Have you heard anything new from the police?"

"No. Not yet."

Confusion shadowed Esme's face as she shook her head. "I was up for most of the night trying to think of anyone who would want to sabotage the grand opening or even carry out the plan as a practical joke gone wrong. It's so unbelievable."

Bea took a plate of lemon-coconut muffins she'd made the other day from the refrigerator. "The police *did* say that there's a good chance we'll never know who's responsible. Without video footage from security cameras or witnesses, they don't have any leads."

A short time later, they sat at the kitchen table with full mugs of coffee and the food.

As Esme unwrapped a muffin, she asked, "Are you up for going over what's happening at the café today, or should we skip it?"

A vision of crawling back into bed and ignoring the world came into Bea's mind. "As long as it's not bad news—sure."

"It's not." Her sister sucked crumbs from her finger as she peered at the calendar on her phone. "The technician from the security company will be at the restaurant between ten and one, and the generator is being serviced at eleven. And they're fixing the window in the office at noon."

Bea sipped her coffee. If the alarm-system install had happened when it was supposed to occur, they wouldn't be discussing any of this. Had the cancellation really been a mistake on the security company's part like they'd all assumed, or had someone actually made that call?

Sighing, she set the questions aside and focused on the present. "Okay. I'll be there."

"No. Freya, Tanya, and I will take care of things," Esme said. "You need a break. And we can handle tomorrow morning's online staff meeting, too."

"I appreciate the offer, but you're getting married next Saturday. You have to get ready for your wedding, and as the boss, I have to be at tomorrow's meeting." Bea squared her shoulders. "The staff needs to hear directly from me that they're getting paid while we're closed. And I still might stop by the restaurant this afternoon. I can't just sit around scrolling through social media and watching cute animal videos all day."

An expression of dread passed over Esme's face so quickly Bea almost missed it. "Yeah, scrolling through social media today probably isn't a good idea."

"Why? Has something been posted about the café?"

As Esme paused to take a sip of coffee, she didn't meet Bea's gaze. "Not really. A few comments were made on the *Chatelaine Daily News* Community Corner, that's all."

Oh no… If bitching and moaning were an art, the people who commented there would win a prize.

Before Esme could stop her, Bea snagged her sister's phone from the table.

"Bea…" she warned. "Seriously, it's not worth reading what they said."

"I need to know what I'm up against." A couple of taps later, Bea pulled up the post about the café. The comments seemed endless.

A complete fail…

This place is permanently off my "must try" list…

The review in the Chatelaine Daily News's online edition is spot-on…

Her heart thumped hard in her chest. "The restaurant critic posted a review?"

"They did? I haven't seen anything. What did they say?"

"I'm afraid to look."

The last time an unfavorable review had been written about a place, it had remained one of the hot topics in town for weeks, and *Don't eat there* had practically become the restaurant's new tagline.

Esme gave her an understanding nod. "Do you want me to read it?"

"No." Bea took a deep breath. "Whatever it is… I can't run from it." She clicked the link, and the review came up on the *Chatelaine Daily News Online*.

> Savory pot pie. Steak with chimichurri sauce. Grilled tilapia with mango salsa. Bourbon-glazed pork chops. Apple fritters topped with ice cream and caramel sauce.
>
> The Cowgirl Café's menu promised mouthwatering goodness, but after so much hype over the past weeks, all it managed to deliver was disappointment with a failed grand opening featuring no food. Should we give them a second chance?

The last line struck like a knife in her chest. Bea handed the phone to her sister.

As Esme read the review, frustration and empathy shone in her eyes. "I'm sorry. I know this isn't what you'd hoped everyone would say. We could reach out to the paper and explain how the opening was sabotaged—"

"We can't. One, it will sound like an excuse, and two, a restaurant mentioning sabotage could make people wonder if the food is safe. But maybe the critic has a point. Why should anyone give me a second chance?" A sad chuckle escaped from Bea. "Are you sure you want me in charge of the food for your wedding? I might ruin that, too."

"First of all, you're *not* responsible for what happened. Whoever broke into the restaurant is to blame. And as far as the wedding? Ryder and I couldn't imagine anyone else catering our reception." Esme grasped her hand. "And more importantly, you deserve all the chances in the world. Opening the Cowgirl Café is important to you. Don't let some anonymous restaurant critic crush your dream."

Hope and determination sparked inside of Bea. "Thank you. I really needed to hear that. But enough about the café. I want to talk about the wedding. You've finalized everything, right?"

"Yes. Working with Lily, as you know, has been amazing." Esme's cheeks glowed with happiness. "I can't wait for next weekend to get here so I can see everything we've talked about come together."

Esme and Ryder's wedding ceremony and reception were being held at the Chatelaine Dude Ranch. It was owned and managed by their brother, Asa, and his wife, Lily.

Lily was organizing the ceremony happening on the lawn behind the spacious event lodge on the property, and the reception taking place afterward inside the lodge.

As Bea listened to Esme gush about all things bridal from dresses to anticipated jitters, a feeling of excitement and joy for her sister made her sit back and smile.

Esme had been there for her with the café. Now was the time to set her own troubles aside and prepare for her little sister's big day.

"That's perfect." The wedding photographer, a brunette dressed in a yellow jumpsuit, snapped candid photos of Esme, Bea, and Lily in the bridal suite located in the lodge at the ranch.

The late afternoon sun shone through a window overlooking a lush green pasture with horses. It gave the cozy bridal suite with a sitting area, makeup table, and curtained-off changing areas a soft glow. It also enhanced Esme's natural radiance and sparkled in her silver jeweled earrings.

Dressed in a pearl-white lace-and-satin gown with an asymmetrical hemline, she beamed the brightest smile out of all of them.

Memories crept into Bea's mind about her own wedding day. Like Esme, she'd been happy. But she'd also had a strong sense of doubt.

No. This wasn't the time for unhappy thoughts.

As Bea pushed the recollection aside, she adjusted the thin shoulder strap on her light coral chiffon knee-length dress. Lily wore the same semiformal attire, and they both had their hair in an artful messy bun.

Lily pretended to fix the white-and-pale-pink flowers adorning Esme's updo. The slender woman with light brown hair, hazel eyes and freckles beamed a smile. "You look so beautiful."

"Thank you." As Esme smiled back at her sister-in-law, she nervously pressed a hand to her stomach. "I can't believe the day is finally here. This all feels like a wonderful dream. Someone might need to pinch me."

As if on cue, Bea and Lily gave Esme's bare arms gentle pinches. The photographer caught the moment along with them laughing about it. As the three Fortune women stared at their reflections in the floor-length mirror on the wall, their expressions shifted to soft smiles.

In her mind's eye, Bea easily imagined Andrea standing with them, beaming a smile and lovingly fretting over if Lars was ready to walk Esme down the aisle. Their parents would have loved Ryder and the grandbabies.

Bea met Esme's gaze in the mirror. From the look on her little sister's face, she'd probably been thinking almost the same things. As Bea rested a hand on her shoulder, they both blinked back tears.

A tragic plane crash had taken Andrea and Lars from them, along with their Aunt Dolly and Uncle Peter. But the love their parents had for them remained.

"Don't you dare cry," Lily warned Esme. "You'll ruin your makeup."

"I know." Esme sucked in a shaky breath as she grasped each of their hands. "But I'm so happy. Thank you for making all this possible."

"You're welcome." Bea held her sister's hand a little tighter.

"And thank *you* both for letting me be a part of this," Lily said.

"You had to be a part of it." Esme smiled brightly. "We're all sisters."

"That's the perfect toast." Bea turned to the side table near the couch where three flutes and a bottle of champagne in a metal ice bucket sat on top of it. She filled the glasses, then handed them to Lily and Esme. "To sisters—family forever."

"Forever," Lily echoed. "And to Esme and Ryder finding true love."

They clinked their glasses, then sipped champagne.

Lily set down her glass. "It's almost time. Bea and I should get out there." Hurrying to the couch, she picked up the beautiful cascade bouquet adorned with purple-

and-white flowers and pale pink roses from a long white box and handed it to Esme. "Asa will be here to get you soon. Are you all set?"

"I'm ready." Esme's eyes sparkled.

Bea and Lily each picked up one of the two smaller round bouquets from the box. After a quick hair and makeup check in the mirror, the two women walked to the door.

On the way out, Bea blew Esme a kiss. "Love you. See you soon."

Moments later, Bea and Lily stood on the lawn a few yards away from a natural jute-burlap aisle runner dividing rows of white wooden chairs in *bride's side/groom's side* configuration.

At the other end sat a white wood gazebo. Pale chiffon and ivy were wound around the columns. Baskets filled with roses, clematis, and hydrangeas in hues mirroring Esme's bouquet hung near the front facing columns forming an arch.

A guitar, cello, and violin trio sitting in the gazebo played a gentle melody.

As Bea looked out at the friends and family there to witness Esme and Ryder's union, her mind drifted back to her own wedding day, over a decade ago in Denver. She and her now ex, Jeff, had met, gotten engaged, and married in a span of less than two months. Their small ceremony with the justice of the peace had been a spur-of-the-moment thing.

None of their family had been able to attend on such short notice, and it had felt so wrong not to have the people she cared about surrounding her on such an important day.

But Jeff had insisted on getting married before they'd

relocated for his job, and wanting to please him, she'd gone along with it. He'd been the man of her dreams.

Shortly after they'd said *I do*, the excitement of newlywed bliss had begun to fade and reality had begun to sink in. Communication wasn't one of Jeff's strong suits. That coupled with Bea, as well as their relationship, coming last in his list of priorities had made it painfully clear their marriage was in trouble. After two years of trying to make the impossible work, she'd divorced him.

Luckily, Esme had gotten it right with Ryder. As a couple, they were all in on continuing to build a strong relationship and family. And it was good to see so many people supporting them. The only ones missing, aside from their parents, were their cousins Bear and West Fortune.

Esme hadn't mentioned it, but she was probably disappointed that Bear hadn't responded to the wedding invite. In fact, no one had heard from him in a long time. Hopefully he was okay and just couldn't make it. And West…

Bea's gaze went to West's former fiancée, Tabitha Buckingham. The young blonde woman in her late twenties sat on the end of a row, tending to her twin babies, Zane and Zach, in their strollers.

West had been a prosecutor. A little over a year and half ago, one of the criminals he had sent to jail had taken West's life. No one in her family had realized Tabitha and the twins existed until the funeral. Now that she lived in the area, they all tried to keep in touch with her. Over the last few weeks, Bea had been meaning to call and check in on her. Tabitha was raising the twins on her own.

Bea glanced down at her dark-haired nephew Chase asleep in the stroller she gently rocked in front of her. He and his brother, Noah, were dressed in midnight-navy suits with pale blush ties like the groomsmen. They looked absolutely adorable.

But unlike his brother, Noah was wide awake in the stroller behind Bea. He was also becoming a little fussy, and Lily was trying to soothe him with a pacifier.

While adjusting her bouquet tucked under the handle, Bea sent up a silent prayer for Chase to remain peaceful while she walked with him down the aisle.

Freya and a temporary nanny seated up front on the bride's side would take over the strollers. They would be watching over the little ones during the ceremony and the reception.

As Bea glanced at the lodge behind them, her attention momentarily halted on the large windows. Inside the building, servers in black-and-white uniforms checked over the tables. Some of them were staff members from the Cowgirl Café, and the rest had been hired from a temp service.

Ryder and Esme had chosen a straightforward sit-down menu: Classic romaine Caesar, choice of grilled flat-iron steak with thyme-and-blue-cheese cream or a seared chicken breast. Both were served with herb-roasted green beans and tomatoes, seasoned rice, and homemade biscuits and honey butter.

Aside from the wedding cake, there were also peach, apple, and pecan tartlets to be served with vanilla cream for dessert.

Having gone over the menu so many times with Tanya, Bea could easily imagine what was happening right now in the lodge's kitchen. All of the food had been safely delivered—she'd double-checked before going to the bridal suite to get dressed for the wedding. By now the cooks should have plated up the salads and prepped their cooking stations.

With this menu, timing was everything, especially with the flat-iron steaks. If they were cooked too long, by the time they were served to the guests, they would be well done and tough. But if they were taken off the grill too soon… What if the cooks couldn't keep up? Esme had trusted her to come up with a great menu. Maybe she'd been too ambitious and should have gone with roast beef instead.

Anxiety twirled in Bea's stomach. No. The menu was solid, and Tanya and the cooks from the café adored Esme. They would do everything in their power to make the meal special.

The musical trio paused, and Bea pushed all other thoughts aside as the minister walked in front of the gazebo.

Moments later, Esme's husband-to-be joined him along with his brother, Brandon, and, Esme and Bea's cousin, Linc Mahoney Fortune. The blond-haired men made a striking trio.

Dressed impeccably in a tailored midnight-navy suit with a pearl-white tie and shirt, Ryder looked just as amazing as Esme. And by the way he kept smoothing his hand down his low-cut vest, he was also nervous.

Brandon briefly rested a hand on his back and murmured something. All three of the men chuckled and Ryder's shoulders relaxed as he took a deep breath.

The trio began playing Pachelbel's "Canon in D."

"That's our cue," Lily said.

After a quick glance down at Chase, Bea went down the aisle, and then Lily followed with Noah.

As planned, they handed off the babies to Freya and the nanny, then took their places. Seconds later, the familiar strains of Wagner's "Bridal Chorus" floated in the air.

Tall, dark-haired Asa, handsome in a suit, walked Esme down the aisle. As she came closer to the front, Esme's gaze locked with Ryder's, and their faces grew luminous as they smiled.

Bea's heart swelled with joy as she held back tears.

The couple shared special passages from books they loved as part of their vows. As they exchanged rings, Chase released a short squeal as if voicing his approval, and everyone laughed.

Their first kiss as husband and wife inspired applause from the guests. On impulse, they scooped up their sons from their strollers. Smiling happily, they walked back down the aisle along with the bridal party to Mendelssohn's "Wedding March."

Following the ceremony, the bridal party greeted the guests on the lawn.

After what seemed like endless hugs and kisses, the line dwindled to the final few.

Devin Street was the last person to congratulate the happy couple. Dressed in a gray suit with a blue tie, he looked scrumptious as usual.

As he chatted with Ryder and Esme, his gaze briefly connected with Bea's. Just like the day of the grand opening, he caught her staring at him and a puzzled look briefly crossed his face. He smiled at her.

Bea glanced down at the bouquet in her hands. She could only imagine what he thought. Either her attraction to him was that obvious or he was thinking about the critic's review of the Cowgirl Café. He was probably trying to figure out how her answer of *Absolutely* when he'd asked if she was ready had been so horribly off the mark.

Suddenly feeling self-conscious, Bea's palms started to sweat. She couldn't face him. Slipping out of line, she spoke to Lily as she handed over her bouquet. "I should go check on the food."

Bea headed for the lodge, certain the tingling along her spine was from Devin watching her as she hurried away.

Chapter Four

Conversation and laughter reverberated in the lodge, and Devin made mental notes of all that was happening from his perspective, seated at a round table for eight in the center of the room.

Luckily he didn't have to remember all the details. The wedding photographer was also freelancing for the *Chatelaine Daily News.* Esme and Ryder had agreed to allow some of the photos to be published along with a brief article he was writing about the wedding.

The lodge was nothing less than impressive. The oak-floored, white-walled space with multiple windows and wood-beam accents had been totally transformed into the perfect venue for the reception.

Guests were seated at tables covered in cream linen and low centerpieces with greenery and white roses. Small trees strung with white lights were nestled near lattice dividers artfully placed in the corners and framing the cake table featuring a three-tiered confection.

One end of the lodge had been delineated as the dance floor, and a DJ played a seamless mix of instrumentals from country to oldies to pop ballads at a low volume.

Esme and Ryder relaxed at a sweetheart table for two,

and the bridal party as well as family members sat at nearby tables around them. But Bea wasn't there.

After the ceremony as he'd spoken to the bridal party in the receiving line, their gazes had locked. She'd looked so gorgeous. He hadn't been able to take his eyes off her and had lost his train of thought while chatting with Ryder. But before he'd gotten a chance to talk to Bea, she'd run off.

Lily had explained that Bea had gone to check on the food for the reception, but a part of him wondered if she might be upset about the review of the Cowgirl Café published in the paper. He'd written the damn thing three times, striving for honesty but not wanting to come across as harsh. That exercise in near futility only proved what he'd tried to deny for a long time. He had a thing for Bea.

He'd wanted to ask her out more than a few times, but he'd hesitated. He was a journalist, after all, and she might think the only reason he was trying to get to know her was because of a potentially big story related to her uncle, Wendell Fortune.

Back in 1965, members of the Fortune family had owned a silver mine near Chatelaine that had collapsed, killing all of the workers. Speculation had always existed about the involvement of Wendell's brothers, Elias and Edgar, in the incident. And recently a question had been raised about the actual number of miners who'd perished. Fifty had been the documented number, but mysterious notes had been found claiming fifty-one lives had been lost.

The arrival of Freya Fortune in Chatelaine with Elias's will—and the claim of him wanting to make amends with his family—had also reinvigorated local interest in the topic.

Who was the fifty-first person, and why point to an additional death now? A couple of months ago, Devin had asked Wendell those questions.

He glanced over at the lean eighty-something older man with a grizzled beard sitting a few tables away with his sister-in-law, Freya. Wendell had said he had nothing to add to the record about the mining disaster, but Devin couldn't shake the feeling that the man was hiding something. And possibly Freya, too.

Mrs. Cofield, an older woman with a silver streak in her dark hair who was seated across from Devin, paused in eating her chicken entrée. She and her husband lived on one of the larger ranches in the area.

She addressed the middle-aged couple next to her. "Wendell Fortune doesn't look well at all. I hardly recognized him when he sat up front before the ceremony."

"You're right—he doesn't look good," the blonde with high-arched brows responded. "I haven't seen him in a while. From what I understand, he's been hiding out in that monstrosity he owns..."

Monstrosity? That was harsh. Wendell's home in town, Fortune's Castle, was elaborate and a little crazy in its medieval design, but Devin didn't think it was an eyesore. And besides, it wasn't in a very populated area where people had to look at it every day.

Holding back the comment, Devin focused on his delicious steak instead of the banter taking place.

"Mr. Street," Mrs. Cofield called out to him, "do you know what's going on with Wendell Fortune?"

He gave her a polite smile. "I'm sorry. I missed what you were saying..."

"Wendell Fortune—have you heard anything about his health?"

"I'm afraid I don't know anything about that." Devin took a sip of iced tea. And even if he did, he'd never reveal that information. He ran a respectable newspaper, not a gossip magazine.

Fortunately, just then, Brandon Hayes tapped his glass diverting attention as he rose from his seat at a table near Esme and Ryder.

He faced the guests. "As part of my speech, I'm supposed to sing my brother's praises and tell you all about his many good points." He looked to the couple with a humorous smile. "Or I can dish the dirt so my new sister-in-law has a really clear picture of what she's gotten herself into..."

He delivered some good-natured teasing, then ended with a heartfelt wish for Ryder and Esme's long and happy future.

During the applause after the toast, Bea came from the back of the room and joined Brandon and the rest of the bridal party.

Devin took note—everyone at the table had a plus-one seated next to them except for Bea. She was smart and beautiful—how could she not have a date for the wedding? Was she on her own because she was busy supervising the catering for the reception?

As the room grew quieter, she rose from her seat and spoke to the newlyweds. "There's a saying about love looking outward in the same direction. When I look at you two, that's what I see..." Bea continued to share a loving, heartfelt recognition of the couple. At the end of her speech, she encouraged everyone to raise their glasses. "To Esme and Ryder."

After the toast, servers delivered trays with an assortment of fruit tartlets to the table.

Mrs. Cofield put one on her plate. "Aren't these on the menu at her restaurant?" She pointed to Bea, who was moving from table to table, chatting with guests. "Considering what happened with the Cowgirl Café, I'm not surprised she's been hiding from everyone. I heard some ridiculous rumor about someone stealing the food."

The blonde sniffed. "She should just own up to whatever really happened. If the place does finally open, I'm not sure I'll ever eat there. She ruined my sister's birthday celebration." She raised her voice, seemingly wanting others to overhear the conversation. "I'm completely on board with the restaurant review in the *Chatelaine Daily News*. I'm not convinced her café deserves a second chance."

That wasn't what he'd said...exactly. Irritation sparked in Devin. Although the restaurant hadn't confirmed anything officially, from what he'd pieced together, whatever had happened wasn't entirely Bea's fault. But this wasn't the time or place to mention the review or the failed grand opening...unless the woman intentionally wanted to hurt Bea's feelings.

The DJ called out, "It's time to bring Mr. and Mrs. Hayes back to the dance floor..."

Esme and Ryder's first dance as a couple had been to a slow song at the start of the reception. Now an upbeat country track played through the speakers.

Bea paused at a nearby table and then headed toward his.

The thought of her smiling at Mrs. Cofield and the

blonde woman without a clue of what they'd been saying about her, and the café, irked him even more.

Devin rose to his feet and intercepted her. "This is the song you mentioned, isn't it?" He grasped Bea's hand. "The one you really wanted to dance to tonight?"

As she glanced up at him, her expression grew perplexed.

He gave her hand a squeeze, willing her to follow along.

To his relief, Bea squeezed back. "You're right. Let's go."

Devin led her to the dance floor. As soon as he took her into his arms, they moved in time to a country two-step.

Bea leaned in, making it easier for him to hear her. "I'm assuming I read the situation right—you needed a save?"

Devin considered his answer. There was no point in telling her the truth and risk ruining her night. "I did. If you hadn't come along, I would have had to fake an injury so I could leave the table."

She quirked a brow. "What type of injury were you going to fake?"

"I don't know. I hadn't gotten that far yet. Maybe a sudden reoccurrence of an old elbow injury from my college football days."

"An old elbow injury?" As she leaned back to look up at him, humor filled her blue eyes and a light flush came into her cheeks. "Aggravated by what? Sitting there eating dinner?"

"Hey, it could happen."

As Bea's laughter radiated into him, he couldn't help but chuckle. The happiness on her face caused his heart to jolt with an extra beat. Damn, she was pretty.

Momentarily distracted, he missed a step. If he didn't

keep his mind on what he was doing, he'd stomp on her coral-painted toes peeking out of her strappy sandals.

Unfazed by his clumsiness, Bea synced her steps with his and settled comfortably in his arms.

More couples came onto the dance floor, and they were pushed closer together. Devin fought the urge to confirm his suspicion that she'd fit perfectly against him.

As she leaned near his ear, the alluring perfume wafting from the curve of her neck intoxicated him. "You're not faking wanting to dance with me, are you?"

Her whispered words, only for him, raised goose bumps on his skin. Devin's heart thumped harder in his chest. "Not a chance."

Chapter Five

Bea felt like she was dancing on air. Was she really this close to Devin right now? Wow. He was gorgeous.

Normally she was tongue-tied around him, but now she couldn't stop flirting with him. It was probably because of the champagne and that she was deliriously happy for Esme and Ryder. And she might've been delirious from hunger, too. She hadn't eaten anything since breakfast. But Bea's need for food faded as her and Devin's hands clasped a bit tighter.

One song moved into the next, and the distance between them started shrinking to mere inches as they moved through the maze of the dance. Devin spun her around, and Bea couldn't wait for the turn to end, anxious to feel his warmth and the solid strength of his arms around her again.

The DJ cued up a slow song, and they didn't hesitate in getting close. As she wound her arms around his neck, he slipped his hands around her waist.

Each gentle sway was a tease as they brushed against one another, until finally she was pressed up against him. Desire warmed inside of her like the first sips of champagne. Savoring the heady feeling, she closed her eyes and reminded herself to breathe.

Devin's shaky exhale feathered along her cheek, and she felt a small shudder move through him.

It was good to know that she wasn't the only one affected.

The melody ended far too soon, and the DJ picked up the pace with a faster song.

Bea and Devin stopped moving, but she remained in his arms at the edge of the floor, out of the way of enthusiastic dancers.

"I'll escort you back to your table." He stepped back and took hold of her hand.

"No…wait. I haven't eaten yet."

Concern furrowed his brow. Before she could explain, he led her off to the side of the room. "You should have said something. I wouldn't have held you up."

"You didn't hold me up. I liked dancing with you…a lot," she confessed. And even though they'd stopped, she wasn't ready for the moment to end.

Going out on a limb, Bea glanced out the window at the gazebo. "We could sit outside." She rushed to explain, "It will feel strange if I'm sitting at the table eating when no one else is." As if it had a mind of its own, her hand tightened a bit more around Devin's.

He brushed his thumb over the back of it, and her heart skipped a beat. "Fix yourself a plate. I'll wait for you outside."

In the lodge's small kitchen, the area was already cleaned up. Most of the staff had departed except for Tanya, who was making one last check for any of the café's supplies, and the scaled-down waitstaff crew.

It was hard to believe that just a few hours ago they'd been in the thick of it, preparing plates for the guests.

"Thank you for doing such a great job. And for this." Bea pointed to the plate in her hand piled high with food.

"I'm so glad we pulled it off." Tanya smiled. "Now people will know what to expect when the Cowgirl Café opens."

I'm not sure I'll ever eat there. She ruined my sister's birthday celebration...

Bea had overheard the remark from the woman at Devin's table. She'd just decided to ignore it and greet everyone with a smile. But then Devin had stood up. As soon as he'd taken her hand, she'd forgotten about the woman's snarky comments. Well...maybe she hadn't completely forgotten. She just didn't care. Dance with Devin, or talk with people who thought it was okay to gossip about her at her sister's wedding? The choice hadn't been that hard to make.

"Oh, and I can't take full credit for the plate," Tanya added. "Make sure you thank Esme for that. She noticed you hadn't eaten and asked me to set aside some food for you."

Warmth flooded through her. Even on her own wedding day, her little sister was looking out for her.

As Bea headed toward the door to join Devin, she passed by the dance floor. She spotted Esme and Ryder, holding each other close. They swayed slowly to their own beat, oblivious to the fast timing of the song and the energetic dancers around them.

They were so lucky to have found each other. A longing for something just as wonderful in her own life hit Bea. Maybe someday...

Outside, the chairs were still set up, and Devin stood in front of the stairs leading to the gazebo.

As she walked toward him, a hint of strange, giddy excitement hit her. She hadn't walked down the aisle at her first wedding. Was this a small glimpse of what that felt like?

He pointed to the structure. "I set up chairs for us. I thought you could use one as a table."

"That's perfect—thank you." She strolled up the stairs, took a seat, and did just as he'd suggested.

Devin put his suit jacket on the back of the chair beside her before taking a seat.

She offered him the extra rolled silverware she'd brought along.

He held up his hand in refusal. "After all the running around you've been doing today plus me making you dance, I know you're starving."

"There's way too much here for one person, and you didn't make me dance with you."

"I kind of did. I ambushed you."

"Yeah, you did." She winked at him. "And the only way I'll forgive you is if you help me eat some of this."

A smile tugged at his mouth. "Well, if it's the *only* way, I guess I don't have a choice." He accepted the silverware. "Actually, you don't have to twist my arm. The food was excellent. I'm looking forward to eating at your restaurant."

"Thank you." The thought emerging in her mind slipped out. "I wish your restaurant critic and your tablemates felt the same way as you do."

"So you *did* hear those women talking. I was hoping you hadn't. You shouldn't have to engage with negativity about the café, especially at your sister's wedding." He paused. "About the restaurant review…"

"No, you're right. Let's not spoil this." On a reflex, she briefly laid her hand on his arm. "I don't want to talk about the grand opening. I'm having a good time right now. I'd rather find out more about you."

What looked to be discomfort flickered in his eyes. Maybe she'd misread their chemistry and Devin was just politely sharing a meal with her. Disappointment set in. Bea prepared to give him an out.

But genuine interest came back into his expression. "Do I get to find out more about you, too?"

"Are you asking me as a journalist?"

"Nope. As me," he replied.

"Then ask away."

His gaze held hers. "Ladies first."

Talking and sharing a meal flowed as easily between them as dancing together.

Favorite songs. Hot or mild salsa. He liked his off-the-charts spicy. Wait. Had she really just confessed her go-to movies were holiday films…all year long? Devin was just so easy to talk to, and watching his smile turn into an unconscious sexy grin was an experience of its own.

He leaned closer as he relayed a story about a Great Dane he'd recently fostered. "I'm sitting on the couch watching the game, eating vanilla ice cream with crumbles of salted-caramel chocolate chip cookies—"

"Hold on. Not just cookies, but *crumbles* of cookies?"

He shook his head. "No. Not just any cookies. Salted-caramel chocolate chip cookies. Crumbling them is the only way for them to perfectly blend with the ice cream. Everyone knows that."

She feigned seriousness. "I didn't, but of course that makes perfect sense…"

He kept a semi-straight face as humor gleamed in his eyes. "Glad I cleared that up for you. So, Chumley starts chasing his tail, like dogs do. Just as I put my bowl on the coffee table to check something on my phone, I see disaster coming. Before I can stop it, he loses his balance and his paw—or maybe it was his tail—hits the bowl, and it flies across the room, slams into the wall, and shatters. Chumley does a duck-and-cover move, then glances up at me with a what-did-*you*-do look on his face. I swear he thought it was my fault."

As Bea laughed with Devin, his sexy grin reappeared, and all she could do was stare at him.

"Something wrong?" he asked.

"No."

In fact, everything felt just right. Maybe a little *too* right. She couldn't remember the last time she'd felt this good with a guy. Or wanted a kiss so badly. The desire to feel his mouth on hers grew into a persistent longing.

As she dragged her gaze upward, she met his gaze. Who leaned in first? She didn't know.

When their lips met, it didn't matter.

One all-too-brief press of their lips turned into a second one. He cupped her cheek, and heat curled inside of Bea as she waited in anticipation. When he angled his mouth back over hers, she opened to him. The heady decadence of the kiss pulled a moan out of her as she grasped onto his forearm, his bicep, then his shoulder, fighting the urge to crawl onto his lap.

Devin eased back. As he let go of her, he stood. "Dance with me."

The switch from kissing to him wanting to dance again confused her. As she stepped into his arms and he brought her close, the mix of need and barely reined in control she spotted in his eyes explained everything.

But she didn't want him to hold back.

As if reading her mind, he rested his forehead to hers. "Bea…it's not that I don't want you, but we shouldn't go beyond that kiss."

"Why?" She leaned away and looked up at his face. "Because you're friends with my brother-in-law? Or because you're a journalist, and my family and I have had some newsworthy events come into our lives?"

Devin smoothed back a strand of red hair that had wandered in front of her eyes. As he took his hand away, a trail of tingles remained where he'd caressed her cheek. "That's a big part of it…"

As he took hold of her waist with both of his hands, she searched for the words to make him see her point of view. She'd taken a bold risk to follow her dream of opening a restaurant in Chatelaine. But when it came to her personal life, she'd kept it on hold for so long. Waiting for what? She didn't know. But she wanted to move forward with what she felt…what she *wanted.*

Bea called upon the boldness that had fortified her choices over the past months. "Whatever that 'big part' is, it doesn't have to affect us being together right now. Why can't we set that all aside, just for tonight?" she asked. "We don't talk about it. We don't worry about it. We just focus on being together and enjoying the moment."

He looked into her eyes. "And after that?"

"Tomorrow, when the sun rises, we get back to reality."

Chapter Six

Devin held Bea's waist a little tighter, fighting the temptation to bring her flush against him and kiss her. If he did, he might not be able to stop.

Lyrics from the song they were dancing to filtered into Devin's thoughts. It was about a guy who'd encountered a woman who'd unexpectedly grabbed his attention, and now he was so caught up in her, he couldn't let her go.

Those words definitely mirrored how Devin felt in this moment with Bea. He hadn't come to the wedding anticipating any of this—especially this connection with her that kept growing by the minute.

She studied his face. "What are you thinking?"

That if he gave in to what he was feeling, he *would* need until sunrise to get Bea out of his system. Maybe one night wouldn't be enough. But on the other hand, if he walked away now, he would have regrets. He really liked Bea. And if one night was all they could have, he would take it.

He caressed up and down her back, and she leaned more against him. "I was wondering how much longer you have to stay at the reception."

"Esme and Ryder should be cutting the cake soon. Shortly after that, they'll leave for their honeymoon," she told him. "Once that happens, there's not much more for me to do, and if there is, I'll figure out a way to move things along. I'll text you before I leave."

He retrieved his phone from his suit jacket and gave it to her. After Bea added her information to his contacts, he called her number.

"Bea..." Esme shouted from across the lawn. "It's time to cut the cake."

"Okay," Bea answered, then looked back to Devin. "Are you coming?"

"Not yet." He needed to cool off.

As Bea started to walk away, he caught her lightly by the hand. She wasn't from Chatelaine, and she'd only gotten a taste of what gossip was like in a small town from what had happened with the restaurant.

He couldn't resist one last reality check. "I'm sure people have noticed us together and they're already speculating about what's going on between us. If you're hurrying to leave the reception, they might figure it out."

Bea came back toward him, rose onto her toes, and gave him a lingering kiss. Just a fraction away, her whispered words warmed his lips. "I know."

Just as she'd predicted, after the cutting of the cake, events at the reception moved along at a steady pace.

Soon, the guests stood in a pasture near the lodge as Ryder and Esme exchanged hugs and kisses with family and close friends. A helicopter waited to whisk them away to the airport to catch a flight.

As the craft lifted off, the couple waved. Everyone waved back, watching until it became smaller and smaller in the sky.

Devin met Bea's gaze across the lawn. Certainty was still in her eyes, and his heartbeat amped up. He couldn't wait to be with her.

Later on, as he knocked on the door of her condo, taking it slow was the plan. But then Bea opened the door. She was still wearing the coral dress. As he took her in, from her long, red hair now loose around her shoulders down to her bare feet, he was more than just caught—he was lost.

He walked inside, and Bea shut the door behind him.

In the next instant, they were in each other's arms, and he gave in to the need to feel her soft, full lips under his. Oxygen became secondary to the ever-deepening kiss that conveyed what they craved for just one night.

Each other.

He'd left his tie and jacket in the car, and Bea took over where he'd left off, unfastening buttons at the top of his shirt. Her moan of frustration vibrated into him, and she gave up, tugging his shirt from his slacks.

With his sleeves already rolled to his forearms, Devin used the advantage and pulled his shirt over his head.

As he tossed it aside, her gaze roamed over his torso.

He worked out and had a toned physique, but maintaining a six-pack had taken a back seat to keeping up with his schedule and raising his daughter. But as Bea glided her hands over his bare skin, her touch ignited a sharp breath, resurrecting a swell of tiny muscles in his abdomen as hard as the solid ridge pressing against the front of his slacks.

Need fired through his blood. But as he brought her close, he took the pace down a notch with long, slow kisses and even slower caresses as he pulled down the zipper on the back of her dress.

Devin eased the straps from her shoulders, and Bea shimmied out of the dress. Coral-colored lace highlighted the combination of her smooth, silky skin, full breasts, and soft curves.

Kissing her, he murmured, "You're beautiful."

As Bea led him up the stairs, the mesmerizing sway of her hips was like a Siren's call, beckoning him to follow.

Urgency fueled them as they took off the rest of their clothing. The breathtaking view of Bea almost made him forget to take condoms from his wallet and lay them on the bedside table.

Moments later, she lay under him, skin to skin. He savored every moan and deep sigh as he pleased her with more caresses and hot, branding kisses.

Holding on to his shoulders, Bea trembled. "Devin… please. I need you."

Pausing briefly, he grabbed protection and put it on.

When he returned to Bea, she reached for him, widening her legs to accommodate him. As he grasped her hips, the wonderful sensation of being inside of her almost overwhelmed him, but he held on to control.

Eyes locked on each other, they moved as one. Entranced by the play of blissful emotion on her face, Devin became driven by as single-minded mission to bring her pleasure.

Bea reached her peak. And soon after he joined her, finding his release.

Later on, instead of leaving, Devin crawled back into bed and held her close. "You good?"

"Very good." Facing toward him, Bea fit like a puzzle piece finding its place.

He shouldn't get too comfortable, right? That's not how a one-night stand worked. He should get dressed and say goodnight.

But being with Bea, holding her…it was too hard to convince himself to leave.

Just after dawn, Bea awoke in Devin's arms. As erotic memories from last night and earlier that morning played through her mind, she couldn't stop a smile. She hadn't experienced anything like being with Devin since…well, she had nothing to compare it to.

"Hey…" His voice was husky from sleep. He wrapped an arm around her and caressed up and down her bare back. "Are you getting up already?"

"Not yet." She snuggled closer to his side and laid her head on his shoulder. As she rested her hand on his chest, the warmth from his skin seeped into her palm.

Just as she was about to ask him if he liked pancakes, a buzz and a ding reverberated from the floor.

"That's my phone. Sorry—I better see who it is." Devin slipped his arm from around her, leaned down, and fished it out of his pants pocket.

She settled back on the pillows. So much for pancakes.

Devin lay back down and checked the screen. "It's my daughter, Carly. She can't find her earbuds, and she's wondering if she left them at my place. She wants to look for them this morning." Sighing, he laid his phone on the nightstand. "Teenage priorities. She never gets up this early for school."

Bea knew he had a daughter but hadn't realized she was a teenager. "How old is she?"

"She'll be fourteen in a few months."

Lying on her side, she faced him. "Raising a teen—I hear that's an interesting experience."

Devin chuckled wryly. "You could say that. But it's also amazing and baffling at the same time. She's growing up and learning how to figure things out for herself. That's the amazing part. But sometimes, trying to understand how a teenage girl's mind works is like trying to solve a puzzle without clues. Almost everything I say or do, these days, is the opposite of what she wants."

Hints of frustration were in his tone, and Bea's heart went out to him. Despite his frustration, the soft rays of sunlight streaming between the slats of the window blinds illuminated parental pride on his face.

She rested a hand on his arm. "When she's older, I'm sure that will change. At least that's what I've heard happens with teenagers."

"I hope it's true." Devin sat up on the mattress. He leaned over and kissed her forehead. "I better get going. Mind if I take a quick shower?"

"Not at all." As she sat up, she tugged at the sheet, holding it to her chest.

Devin's gaze dropped from her face to the curves of her breasts still peeking above the covers, and he swallowed hard.

A part of Bea was tempted to let the sheet drop and go for round three. But he probably wanted to get home and change out of yesterday's clothes before meeting his daughter.

Pulling the sheet up higher, she asked, "Do you want coffee?"

Devin cleared his throat. "That would be great."

She gave him a clean towel and one of the pre-pasted toothbrushes she kept on hand for travel. After finding out how he wanted his coffee, she put on a sleep shirt, made a pitstop in the other bathroom, then went downstairs.

A short time later, Bea climbed back up the stairs carrying two full mugs of dark Colombian brew. As she slowed down, making sure not to spill hot coffee, she glanced down at the mugs and smiled. She and Devin weren't just sexually compatible. They even liked their coffee the same way—a couple of teaspoons of sugar, no cream.

That would have been a good sign…if they were at the start of a relationship. But they weren't. She had a restaurant to run, and he had a teen daughter to raise. They were on different paths.

Still, Bea's mind started to wander, imagining what might happen next if those different paths converged, even for just a few more days. Would they meet up later and spend the rest of the day together? Then would they explore possible plans to see each other for the rest of the week or maybe a bit longer? As long as they both knew an end was in sight…

As she walked into the bedroom, Devin walked out of the bathroom wearing just a blue towel around his waist.

Her thoughts short-circuited as want curled in her belly.

As he walked toward her, drops of water glistened on his muscular chest. She couldn't tear her gaze away as a few droplets slid down his abdomen toward the edge of the towel.

"Bea…"

His voice snapped her out of a trance, and she looked up. Blatant need was in his eyes.

Devin slipped the mugs from her hands, set them on the dresser, then came back to her. Taking her by the waist, he brought her close.

"But your coffee..." The three-word question was all she could manage to say.

"It can wait." Devin leaned in. "This can't."

He slanted his mouth over hers.

In short order, his towel and her sleep shirt were on the floor. As he cupped her bottom, Devin brushed open-mouthed kisses along the sensitive skin of her throat. The evidence of his desire nestled against her belly. Holding tightly to his shoulders, she wound her legs around his waist as he swiftly carried her to the unmade bed.

Every touch, kiss, and caress reflected all she felt. Impatience and pure need. By the time he entered her, she was trembling and nearly lightheaded with anticipation. Each swift, hard stroke delivered more and more pleasure until she splintered apart in ecstasy.

Depleted from his own orgasm, Devin rose to his elbows supporting his weight. "You okay?"

Floating in contentment, Bea smiled as she stroked a hand up and down his back. "I'm wonderful."

He stared into her eyes. "I'm sorry I can't stay longer."

"Me, too." But maybe it was better this way. If he hung around for coffee and breakfast liked she'd imagined, it would have been harder to watch him leave.

Devin moved away from Bea and sat on the edge of the bed with his back to her. He moved to get up but stopped, staring between his legs. "Damn," he whispered.

Hearing concern in his tone, she grasped the sheet to her chest once more and sat up. "What's wrong?"

He glanced over at her. "The condom broke."

Still processing what had occurred earlier in the bedroom, Bea stood with Devin at the kitchen counter holding on to her coffee mug. For her, having the cup in her hand was a nervous gesture more than a need for caffeine.

They'd waited until coming downstairs to discuss what had happened. She'd never fully understood the saying about cutting through tension with a knife until now. It filled the room along with a heavy silence.

Devin sat down his full mug. "I'm sorry. I should have noticed..."

She couldn't let him take all the blame. "We were caught up in the moment. It's not your fault."

As she reached for his hand on the counter, he reached for hers, too.

Devin released a heavy exhale. "This isn't how I imagined this morning would end."

"Me neither."

His fingers tightened around hers as he looked into her eyes. "Whatever happens next, I'm here."

Chapter Seven

Bea, Freya, and Tanya sat at a table in the empty café. The topic of their Tuesday-morning meeting was the rescheduled grand opening happening next week.

But Bea's mind kept wandering back to her off-the-charts sexual encounter with Devin a little over a week ago…and how it had ended.

If her cycle wasn't so irregular, she might have been able to count days to get an idea if she'd been in the pregnancy window. But with the added stress of opening the restaurant, her cycle had been even more erratic than usual. And based on her history, there was more than just a good chance she *wasn't* pregnant. Maybe she should have told that to him. He'd looked so concerned before he'd left to meet his daughter.

The next day, he'd sent a text checking in to see how she was doing, and again a few days later. Both times she'd texted back that she was fine. They hadn't communicated since then. But why would Devin reach out again? He was probably waiting to hear news from her. After all, their intent *had* been a one-night stand.

"The key is to not focus on what didn't work but concentrate on what did," Freya said.

The comment brought Bea back into the conversation.

That was a good point. Focusing on what hadn't worked would only lead to worry. Why not just remember how good things had been between her and Devin before the moment had gone sideways?

But her hookup with Devin wasn't what Freya was talking about.

"You're right." Bea slipped off the lightweight gray cardigan she'd paired with a blue shirt and black jeans. "We have to do all we can to promote this opening in a way that will encourage people to rebook their reservations."

"And our plan of offering a free item to the first fifty who do will help with that," Tanya added. "But maybe the options should just be a dozen biscuits to go or a dessert. I think the biscuits will be popular, and food-cost wise, they're a lot cheaper than our appetizers."

Freya smoothed a strand of ash-blond hair from her cheek. "I think either will work as long as we aren't sabotaged again." She frowned. "That's such a terrible thing that happened. I couldn't imagine even conceiving something like that. Could you?" She looked between Bea and Tanya.

"None of us could," Bea replied. "But like you said, we should focus on the positives. And that means we probably shouldn't use the word *sabotage* to describe what happened." Earlier, she'd heard Freya using the word liberally while booking reservations on the phone. "We've come up with a good plan. That's our focus, and now we just have to implement it."

"True." Freya tapped on her tablet. "Lily's idea to have everyone share their photos of Esme and Ryder's wedding has really paid off. She's uploaded them to a site. I know we're supposed to be talking about business, but you have to take a peek."

The wedding was definitely a bright spot. And from Esme's text message a few days ago, she and Ryder were enjoying their extended honeymoon at a resort in the Maldives. And they were looking forward to the nanny bringing Chase and Noah to join them.

Bea accepted the tablet from Freya. Many of the photos showed the couple gazing lovingly at each other, even the candid ones when they weren't aware someone was watching them. And there were several cute pics of their baby boys as well.

Freya pointed. "This one of you and Devin is really nice."

The person taking the photo had captured Devin as he was about to spin Bea around. They were smiling at each other. Memories of happiness along with remembered desire curled through her.

She'd told Devin that she didn't have time for a relationship of any kind. But honestly, if things had ended differently after their night together, she would have been tempted to see him again.

A knock sounded at the front door.

Tanya stood. "That's probably Mrs. Lansing. I'll let her in."

"I'll do it." Freya gathered up her things. "I'm on my way out anyway. I have errands to run."

"Okay, thanks." Tanya turned to Bea. "There's a delivery coming in. I'll be in the kitchen if you need me."

Moments later, Bea sat at the table with the thirty-something brunette dressed casually in blue active wear. She'd spoken to Esme a few weeks ago about the possibility of booking the café for a private event.

"Please, call me Sophia." The woman's cheeks flushed

pink as she became the equivalent of an octopus, giving her baby a pacifier and setting up her five-year-old son, Easton, with a coloring book all while wrangling her daughter, a toddler named Amelia. "Apologies for bringing the kiddos along. My sitter woke up sick this morning and couldn't look after them. I just didn't want to cancel our meeting."

"That's perfectly okay. Can I get you anything?"

"No, I'm good. Thank you." After settling Amelia on her lap, Sophia snagged an adult water bottle for herself and a matching kiddie water bottle for the toddler. "So, I'm planning a fiftieth wedding anniversary celebration for my in-laws…"

They chatted about several ideas for the Sunday late-morning event.

Bea drew out a rough sketch of the room layout for the party on her tablet. "Not going with a plated meal actually opens quite a few options. We can set up a buffet line, and we can also set up separate omelet and Belgian waffle stations here and here. And even a dessert station if you like." She looked up from her tablet to smile at her client. "You mentioned all the grandkids would be attending. Make-your-own ice cream sundaes could be fun."

"We get to have ice cream?" Five-year-old Easton flashed a grin, revealing a missing front tooth.

Amelia squealed at him.

"Maybe." Sophia smiled. "Ice cream sundaes are actually a great choice. My mother-in-law used to work at an ice cream shop in high school. My father-in-law was the stud quarterback, and he used to stop by to flirt with her. All these years later, they still act like teenage sweethearts."

"Aww. That's wonderful."

"It is." Sophia leaned away as Amelia waved her arms, spraying drops of water from the attached straw on her bottle. "And they had six kids." Giving in to Amelia squirming around, she let the child slide from her lap. "Honestly, I don't know how Joan did it. My husband and I barely had a handle on things with two kids when Corbin snuck up on us."

"Snuck up?" Bea smiled brightly at the toddler who came over and grasped on to her fingers.

The weight of Amelia's hand in hers was almost nothing, but the light in the little girl's hazel eyes declared, *I'm here. I know you see me. I see you.*

"*Snuck up* is probably the wrong choice of words." Sophia laughed. "Hubby and I went to Acapulco for a long weekend to celebrate our anniversary, and the result was Corbin." She glanced at the baby sleeping in the stroller. "He was absolutely unexpected. A word from the wise—even the best protection fails."

A short time later, they wrapped up their meeting and Bea walked Sophia and her children to the door. But Sophia's warning about her Acapulco trip remained on Bea's mind.

Her morning with Devin couldn't have resulted in the unexpected? *Could it?*

The question haunted her the rest of the day. On the way home, she gave in to the impulse and drove to GreatStore. The big-box retailer sold everything from groceries to clothes to home goods and personal items…including pregnancy tests.

Inside the store, she grabbed a handheld shopping basket and headed for the personal-care section.

She perused the myriad of test boxes. The packaging

on some of them had changed from years ago, but they were still familiar. Rapid results, countdown clocks, pregnancy test strips, a triple-check test proclaiming it offered even more reassurance about the result.

A fleeting recollection played through her mind of buying multiple tests years ago. At times, when she'd used them, it had almost felt as if she was playing the pregnancy lottery, hoping for the winning result. But it had never happened.

A customer passing by jostled Bea from her thoughts. She didn't recognize the woman curiously staring at her, but what if she had? Or what if Freya or Asa and Lily or one of the staff at the café walked by and saw her looking at pregnancy tests? What would she tell them?

Heart thumping from a sudden surge of anxiety, she grabbed a "six days or sooner" test kit along with another kind as a backup and quickly left the aisle. On a reflex, she snagged two pairs of neon-colored moisturizing socks and piled them on top of the tests along with packages of deodorant and a large value-size bodywash from the next aisle.

Moments later, she stood in the "twenty items or less" self-checkout line, praying she wouldn't run into anyone she knew.

After what felt like forever, she finally reached the register. Nervousness made her hands a tad unsteady as she dug out the tests first and scanned them on the reader.

If Esme were around, Bea would have called her for support. She didn't know Lily well enough to tell her, but she wouldn't want to burden her with keeping this type of a secret from Asa. If he found out, he'd leap into big-brother protective mode and maybe even call Devin, demanding to know his intentions.

Farther down, a familiar-looking guy entered the store. The bodywash she was scanning almost slipped out of her hands. Had thinking of her one-night stand conjured up his presence? No, of course not. It was just a small town.

Devin paused in the main aisle and glanced at his phone.

Whatever happens next, I'm here...

Recalling what he'd said brought a sense of comfort. If she told him how nervous she was about taking the test, would he empathize with her? Or maybe even be there when she took it? A large part of her believed he would. But she couldn't just walk up to him in the store and ask. But she did have his number. She could call him from the parking lot.

As Bea hurried to pay for her things, a teenage girl joined Devin. He smiled at the girl as they walked in the opposite direction.

Was that Carly?

A sense of isolation hit Bea. Devin had other important priorities. She would have to face this next step on her own.

Chapter Eight

Devin inched his black truck forward in the trailing line of cars headed to the front of the middle school. As he flipped down the visor, blocking out most of the morning sun, he stifled a yawn.

Carly sat beside him in the front passenger seat of the crew cab, munching on cinnamon French toast sticks while texting on her phone.

Yesterday she'd stayed after school for a club meeting. Lauren had had to work late and couldn't pick her up, so he'd taken his daughter to his place for the night. At GreatStore, while they'd been shopping for the items to make spaghetti for dinner, she'd put the box of toast sticks into the basket.

Lauren was a health nut and wouldn't approve of Carly eating what she deemed the equivalent of junk food first thing in the morning. But from the way the thirteen-year-old was gobbling the toast sticks, she'd needed a break from the choices of muesli, quinoa, raisin bran, or Greek yogurt with fruit for breakfast.

But he *had* fed her a balanced meal last night. Spaghetti with meat sauce and a salad. Carly had sliced up the vegetables for the salad, and he'd made everything else. While they'd prepared the meal, she'd talked to him about her homework. One of her last assignments of the school year was to write an essay on a social issue affecting teens. She hadn't chosen a topic yet.

The impact of social media on mental health, peer pressure, bullying, addiction... While he was proud of her knowledge on those subjects, their conversation had made him acutely aware of the things she was facing at her young age.

Despite questioning his and Lauren's parental wisdom at almost every turn, Carly was staying on the right path, choosing independence and responsibility instead of caving to the wrong influences. He was proud of her.

It was hard to believe that soon she would finish eighth grade. And that coming fall, when he drove her to school, he would have to drop her off on the other end of the campus at the high school entrance.

Carly caught him looking at her, and teen wariness reflected on her face. "Why are you staring at me like that?"

"Like what?" he said.

"Like you're wondering about me."

"And that's a bad thing?"

Carly's silent raised brow before she turned her attention back to her phone conveyed her answer.

Moments later, they were at the designated drop-off zone.

She grabbed her backpack from the floor. "Bye, Dad."

Not wanting to embarrass her by making a "big deal" about the quick kiss she gave him on the cheek before she got out, he held back a grin until after he'd driven off.

Next stop was the Saddle & Spur Roadhouse to pick up the pastries and sandwiches he'd ordered from the restaurant. He and his staff were putting together the Sunday edition that was due to the printer, and they would be tied to the office until the late afternoon. An endless supply of food and coffee was a must.

As he exited the school's campus, he turned up the radio. The last song he and Bea had danced to under the gazebo played through the speakers.

Maybe he should reach out to her again? But when he had, she'd said she was okay, and hearing from him now could be an unwanted distraction. After all, Bea *was* in the midst of preparing for the rescheduled grand opening.

He'd been debating whether he should show up for it as the anonymous critic. Giving an unbiased review of the café would be a challenge for him now. Especially since he felt guilty about her not knowing he'd written the review. In hindsight, he should have insisted on telling Bea up front, but letting go of everything and spending one carefree night together had been too hard to walk away from…and so had the morning after.

But if he'd left like he'd intended right after his shower, things would have ended with the two of them remembering how much they'd enjoyed being together, instead of worrying about possible life-altering changes.

His phone rang through the car's speaker system. But it wasn't Bea. He answered the call.

"Hey, Lauren."

"Hi, Devin. Are you on your way to work?"

"Not yet. I just dropped Carly off at school. I have to pick up some takeout before I head to the office. But before I forget—Carly and I went shopping last night, and she picked out some clothes. The bags are in the car with me. Do you mind if I let myself into the garage so I can drop them off before I head to the Saddle and Spur?"

"Actually, I'm still at home. I was hoping you might be able to stop by this morning so we could talk. Do you have a few minutes?"

Lauren sounded a little off. Was something going on with Carly?

Devin headed for the busy four-lane road just outside of town. "Be there in twenty minutes."

He arrived at Lauren and Carly's house a short time later and backed into the driveway.

When they'd all moved to Texas, the three-bedroom house with wood floors, high ceilings, and a loft over the garage had been their perfect dream home. And Carly loved her space. Over the years, she'd helped paint the walls in her new favorite color of the moment ever since she'd been able to use a paint brush and not make too much of a mess. After the divorce, it had made sense for him to move into a smaller place and his ex-wife and daughter remain there.

As he walked up the stone path carrying the shopping bags with Carly's new things, Lauren opened the front door. She was dressed for work in a gray blouse, slacks and heels.

He left the bags in the entryway, then followed her to the kitchen. Devin sat on a stool on the living room side of the beige granite island.

Lauren selected two glasses from an upper cabinet. "Orange juice good?"

"Sure. Thanks."

She took a container out of the refrigerator, poured him a glass, then spooned up some quinoa from a pot on the stove into a bowl. She set both in front of him.

He wasn't into quinoa, and Lauren knew that. Yeah,

something was *definitely* off. Devin nudged the bowl aside. "So what's up?"

Lauren took her time pouring a glass of orange juice for herself. "Last night at work, there was a conference call with the higher-ups in the company. They announced that they're downsizing."

Was she at risk of losing her job? As a claims-department supervisor at an insurance company, she'd been climbing the ranks to a management position. He could only imagine how Lauren felt after receiving the bad news.

But her company, located in the next town over, wasn't the only one making big changes. In fact, the paper was publishing an article in the upcoming edition about the economic impact caused by the unexpected exodus of businesses from the area.

"I'm sorry," he said. "I know this is something you hadn't anticipated."

"No." She released a dry chuckle. "It definitely came out of the blue."

Luckily the house was already paid off and so was Lauren's car. As far as he knew, food, utilities, and incidentals were her main concerns.

"If you're worried about paying the bills, don't be. If you lose your job, I can cover expenses here until you find another one. Just let me know how much you need."

"Actually, they offered me a lateral promotion with a raise." Lauren carefully put down her still-full glass. "I can stay here in my new position…or I can go to Dallas or Corpus Christi."

She'd mentioned all three opportunities. That meant she was weighing all the options. "What did you decide?"

"I chose Corpus Christi. I start there in three months."

She was moving? This was sudden, but it wasn't an unmanageable situation.

Devin took a sip of orange juice and a moment to collect his thoughts. "Okay. Not a problem. Carly has volleyball camp and some volunteer activities lined up for the summer. I can adjust my schedule. I guess the big question is what do you want to do with the house? If it comes down to it, I could sell my place, and that way Carly could stay put."

Lauren gave him a baffled look. "Carly's not staying here, Devin. She's coming with me. Of course, you'll see her. We'll have to work out weekend visits and which holidays she'll spend with you."

"Hold on. Her friends are here. She's been with some of them since grade school, and all they've ever talked about is attending high school together. And she's planning to try out for the freshman volleyball team or maybe taking up cheerleading again." He met her stare with a hard one of his own. "You can't just yank her away from all of that. This is her *home*."

"I'm not yanking her away from anything." Lauren shook her head. "She'll still be in contact with her friends. And she can join the volleyball team or the cheerleading squad at her new school in Corpus Christi. In fact, their volleyball team has made the regional or state championships for the past five years."

"Her *new* school. So you've already made up your mind. Don't I have a say in it? And what about what Carly wants? Doesn't that count for anything?"

"Of course what Carly wants counts." Lauren threw up her hands. "But we have to be realistic. All those activities she wants to get involved in—if she stays here, who's going to take her back and forth to them? You say you're going to adjust your schedule, but how long will that last? You barely have time for her now."

Irritation prickled over him as he stood. "That's not true."

"How much time has she spent holed up with you in your office because you're working? Or babysitting another puppy you volunteered to foster while you're working? Or tagging along with you on researching a story you're writing? Even the father-daughter-meal outings you take her on are work related. Carly knows you're reviewing the restaurant."

"How?" he demanded. "Because you told her?"

"No. Carly's the one who told me. She started noticing a review from the 'anonymous' restaurant critic appeared in your paper right after she went to the place with you. And you don't have to worry about her telling anyone. She thinks your little secret is exciting."

Carly keeping his secret was the last thing he was worried about. He was worried about losing his daughter. "I can't change the past, Lauren, but if Carly was living with me, there wouldn't be any scheduling problems. I would make it work."

His ex crossed her arms over her chest. "And if you can't, then what? According to our agreement, she's supposed to spend two weeks and two weekends a month with you. That hardly ever happens."

"You make it sound like Carly isn't my priority."

"She is—along with running the newspaper and chasing the next headline story."

Déjà vu hit with her last comment. It was a near repeat

to what Lauren used to say during their arguments before they'd decided to get a divorce.

From the look on Lauren's face, the same realization had crossed her mind. "I don't want to fight about this. I just want what's best for our daughter."

"And so do I." Devin released a measured breath. "But we won't be able to decide what's best for her if we're dragging our past into it. We have to consider *all* sides of this decision. And that includes exploring the possibility of her staying here with me."

"You're right…we have to work this out for Carly's sake. She shouldn't see us divided on this. We also need to work out our differences before we approach her about what's going on."

"I agree. This is our problem, not hers." Grimness entered his tone. "It upsets her when we're not getting along. The last thing we should do is stress her out."

"At least we're on the same page about that, but as far as the rest…" Lauren uncrossed her arms. Her expression shifted from stubbornness to resignation. "There's only one way for us to solve things."

Devin drove into the parking lot of the Saddle & Spur Roadhouse. As he pulled into a vacant spot, his earlier conversation with Lauren, along with her accusations, played through his mind.

He couldn't imagine not having Carly in Chatelaine and only seeing her on weekends or select holidays. And yes, according to the agreement they had now, despite equal custody, she often didn't spend the two weeks and two weekends a month with him. But that wasn't because he didn't *want* her with him.

They knew Carly saw Lauren's place as home. And that made sense considering the three of them had once lived there as a family. They'd adopted a *three weeks there, one week at his place* schedule, and everyone had been happy. But if their daughter wanted to spend a few extra days or weekends in one place or another or wanted to pop by to see him, neither he nor Lauren objected.

His ex-wife throwing in the informal agreement change like it was a negative was more than just a little unfair considering they'd made the adjustment for a good reason. And she shouldn't have just sprung her decision on him. But the fact that she already had a high school picked out for Carly made Devin wonder if this move to Corpus Christi had been in the works for a while.

Yes, she had a right to excel in her career, but when it came to their daughter's welfare, it was a joint effort, not a singular one. And as far as him being able to balance his work schedule and look after Carly, he already had the perfect blueprint on that. His father had done it while raising him as a single parent.

Outside the truck, Devin locked it with the key fob and headed toward the restaurant. At least he and Lauren agreed on one thing. Just like they had with their divorce and the original custody agreement, they were using a mediator to reach an amicable decision.

As he walked past a four-door sedan to the left, he did a double take. *Bea...*

She was just about to open the driver's side door when her gaze met his. "Devin…hi."

"Hello." He walked over to her.

Dressed in black jeans, a white blouse, and a short tan jacket, her appearance was casual yet professional. And she looked pretty as usual.

Standing in front of each other, she seemed as unsure as he felt about how they should greet each other. They leaned in at the same time for a hug.

He breathed in her light floral fragrance, and any awkwardness he'd felt before melted away. Familiarity and sense of rightness replaced it, tempting him into holding her a bit longer.

They released each other.

Meeting her gaze, Devin debated what to say. He couldn't ask if she'd taken a pregnancy test yet. "How are you?"

"Good, but busy." Bea's smile curved up her mouth, but it didn't light up her face. Adjusting the purse strap on her shoulder, she looked at the restaurant. "The owner here has some extra tray racks he wants to get rid of. He called to see if I was interested in them. They're practically brand new."

"So are you interested in them?"

"Yes. We need them. Some of ours were…lost." As she looked up at him, uncertainty briefly shadowed her face, and she looked just as lost. "I should go." She headed back to her car. "See you, Devin."

"Bye, Bea."

He hadn't known her long at all, but he could sense something was off with her. Was he just picking up on the stress she was under with the café, or was it something else?

His phone rang. It was Quinn. She and Charles were probably wondering where he was.

Turning toward the Saddle & Spur, he answered the call.

“Devin, wait…” Bea called out. “I’m pregnant.”

Chapter Nine

I'm pregnant... The confession had just flown out of her mouth. Hearing herself say the actual words that had drummed in her mind all last night felt surreal.

As Devin turned to face her, he spoke into the phone. "I'll call you back."

And she'd not only just told Devin, but most likely whoever he'd been on the phone with had heard it, too. Along with the guy she hadn't noticed walking past them.

The realization of her announcement, including the fact that her life was about to change in a huge way, made it hard to breathe. *Oh, shit...*

He came to her side and wrapped an arm around her. "You're okay. Take a deep breath. Good. Take another."

Devin guided her to his truck. Once she was inside the front passenger seat, he went to the driver's side, got in, and snagged a small bottle of apple juice sitting in the middle console.

He cracked it open. "Here—drink some of this."

Bea accepted the bottle. She took a sip, and the feeling of lightheadedness started to fade. Fine sand-colored granules stuck to her fingers.

Devin noticed her staring at her hand. "It's cinnamon sugar from French toast sticks. Carly was eating breakfast in the car on the way to school this morning." He opened the glove box, took out napkins, and traded them for the bottle.

Making sure his daughter had breakfast on the way to dropping her off at school, apple juice and napkins at the ready… There was no doubt in her mind that the strong, confident man sitting beside her was a natural parent. But as for her? She had no idea where to start in becoming one.

"Feeling better?" he asked.

"Yes, thank you." She balled the napkin in her hand. "I didn't mean to drop the news on you like that—or for whoever you were on the phone with to hear it along with that guy walking through the parking lot. Please tell me you don't know him."

"I don't." Devin studied her face. "And even if I did, I don't care what he heard. Now will you please answer me truthfully. How are you? And where are you in your thinking about being pregnant?"

Bea sorted through her whirling emotions. "I feel like I've been put in a scrambler and shot back out of it. I'm shocked and overwhelmed." The sincerity in his gaze prompted her to be even more honest. "And I'm a little frustrated this didn't happen to me sooner." She responded to his questioning look. "Eight years ago, when I was married, I tried to have a baby…but I couldn't conceive. I'd given up on the possibility of ever getting pregnant."

"And now you are." Devin glanced away with a pensive expression.

"And what about you." Bea balled the napkin tighter in her fist. "How are you feeling about this…honestly?"

His chest rose and fell with a breath. "I'm shocked, too.

I've been in this situation of becoming a parent before, but this is different."

Different... She read between the lines, imagining what he wasn't saying. Back then, he'd been in a committed relationship with someone he'd cared about. "I'm not expecting anything from you. I want this baby, but I know having another child isn't necessarily what you want."

Devin met her gaze. "I didn't say that."

"You just said this situation is different."

"Different in that I'm not in my early twenties trying to get a foothold in my career while becoming a new parent," he clarified. "I have experience. Which is why I won't let you go through this alone."

She shook her head. "I don't want us to feel forced to be together. Or for you to feel trapped. Let's be honest… we don't know each other."

Devin wrapped his hand around her closed one. "No, we don't know each other that well. And I don't know what it's like to be pregnant, but I *do* know going through the changes of pregnancy can be a lot, mentally and physically, especially for a first-time mom. And, of course, I want to know my child. And that includes getting to know you, Bea." As he turned more toward her, he held her hand a little tighter. "I don't want you to be alone or even feel that you're on your own in this—financially, emotionally, or on any other level. It will be easier if you let me be there for you."

Seeing his earnest expression lifted some of the heaviness that had started weighing on Bea that morning. She really didn't want to go through the experience alone. She'd gotten a taste of that in her past marriage.

She and her ex had tried for a long time to get pregnant.

When it hadn't happened, she'd been open to other avenues, but Jeff hadn't been. If she couldn't have a baby "the old-fashioned way," he'd told her, then he hadn't wanted one. The past memory played through her mind. If *she* couldn't have a baby… He'd actually said that.

That comment had finally awakened her to what she'd refused to see. Jeff hadn't been physically or emotionally there for her—and not just with their fertility issues. She'd been the one who'd given everything. All he'd given was promises he'd never kept. He also hadn't understood what she'd needed from him as a husband. And he hadn't been willing to make changes to sustain their marriage.

What Devin offered was the opposite of that. But what if he couldn't keep *his* promises? What if she put her faith in him and he bailed on her, too? She couldn't go through that again, especially with a baby on the horizon.

Bea met Devin's gaze. "I have to be up front with you—I appreciate you wanting to be supportive, but I'm anxious about it, too. You already have a responsibility to Carly. You also run a business. Adding in me and the baby will add more to your already busy life. I don't want to set you up for failure by expecting too much from you."

"It's a legitimate concern. And since you were honest with me, I should be honest with you as well." Grimness shadowed his face. "I just found out this morning that Lauren—Carly's mom—accepted a transfer to Corpus Christi for her job. And she wants to take Carly with her."

Bea's heart went out to him. Devin had probably still been reeling from the news when she'd dropped her bombshell revelation on him. But despite that, he hadn't hesitated in looking after her.

Even though she'd had no way of knowing that her timing was bad, a hint of guilt still rippled through her. Sighing, she relaxed her grip on the napkin, allowing Devin to grasp her hand. "I'm sorry. I know that must have been tough to find out."

He huffed a breath. "Yeah, I definitely didn't see that coming. We've decided to go through mediation instead of the courts to come up with a decision. We've worked things out this way before. Hopefully we can do it again. We just have to remember what's best for Carly."

"That's an important focus." And one she didn't want to get in the way of.

"It is. I'll have to be available to attend sessions with the mediator. And when we tell Carly what's happening with her mom and the move, I'll need to be there to help her process the situation. But that doesn't mean I can't be there for you and the baby, too. I just have to balance my time."

But it wasn't just about time. How would his daughter take the news about the baby? And would the pregnancy negatively impact his position when it came to negotiating the new custody arrangement for his daughter?

Bea held back in asking the questions. Devin had just found out he was about to become a father again along with the prospect of spending less time with his daughter. He hadn't had time to figure all that out yet. And just like she needed support, he probably did, too.

"I appreciate you telling me what's going on with your ex and Carly. You and I being honest with each other puts us on the right course."

"There's something else I need to tell you." A look of regret came over Devin's face. "I'm the newspaper's anonymous restaurant critic."

Chapter Ten

In the *Chatelaine Daily News* office's main conference room, Devin, Charles, and Quinn sat at the large rectangular table reviewing a draft of Sunday's newspaper on their tablets and laptops. The program they used allowed them to make changes in real time so they could all see and comment on adjustments.

As Devin scanned the pages, one thought shadowed the rest in his mind. *Bea was pregnant.*

After their night together, he'd realized that was a possibility, but hearing her say the words was a whole other reality.

She'd looked so anxious. Assuring her that everything would be okay had been important to him. And he would live up to his promise to be there for her. But was he ready to be a dad again?

His heart thumped a little harder as he released a pent-up exhale. He and Lauren had planned having Carly. And as a married couple, bringing a child into the world had been a natural next step for them.

He and Bea weren't even close to ready for this. And they had to find a way to get there. Starting with her forgiving him.

The hurt look on Bea's face that morning after he'd

confessed to writing the review about the café played in his mind.

I'm not holding it against you for not telling me, Devin. I was the one who suggested we set everything aside. But that doesn't erase the fact you encouraged people to question if they should give my restaurant another chance... I don't know how I'm supposed to feel about this. I need time...

That was what she'd told him before she'd gotten out of his truck. She'd also mentioned she'd contact him when she was ready. He could have mentioned that by not being transparent about what had happened at the café on opening night, she'd missed the opportunity for there to be a balanced view on her situation.

But that thinking was from the outside point of view of a journalist and restaurant critic. Not Bea's...what? Just the father of her baby? Had his admission relegated him to only that role in her life? Discontent and concern tugged in his gut. He didn't just want to know his baby, he wanted to get to know Bea.

When they'd been at the wedding reception, they'd shared a natural connection that hadn't been merely on a physical level. A part of him believed that even though they had put a one-night limit on being together, they still would have linked up again. Their connection might have grown into something more. Wasn't that part of their relationship worth exploring, especially now that they were expecting a child together?

The front door chimed in the reception area, jarring him from his thoughts.

Quinn got up and breezed out of the room. The brunette

in her early forties never slowed down, even when she was seated. She just moved from task to task with a fluid ease.

Charles slid his glasses farther up his nose, took a sip of coffee, and kept working. In the midst of calm or chaos, the bald-headed managing editor always retained an intense focus.

Moments later, Quinn popped her head in the door. "Devin—someone's here to see you."

Was it Bea? Hope made him sit up straight in the chair. "Who is it?"

"A woman named Morgana—she said you two spoke over the phone?"

Masking disappointment, Devin sat back in the chair. "We did. But she's early. We're not meeting until later this afternoon."

"Go ahead." Charles chimed in. "Quinn and I can handle this."

Considering how his mind was wandering, it was probably best to turn it over to them. Devin looked to Quinn. "Show her to my office, please. I'll be there in a minute."

After briefly discussing a layout issue with Charles, Devin left the conference room and headed to his office two doors down.

Charles's office was located on the opposite side of the main floor, and Quinn's desk was in the adjoining reception area.

The remaining offices bordering the square-shaped space were empty, along with the four desks in the middle of the room.

Years ago, the office had been occupied by full-time reporters, advertising sales reps, photographers and assistants. An electric energy had buzzed through the building, especially during the pre-publication phase of the paper. But those days were gone forever. Printed newspapers were dying out in favor of online resources.

Now freelance reporters came in and temporarily occupied a desk when they were writing a story for the paper. Or when Carly was there, she would set up camp and do her homework while waiting for him to finish for the day.

Devin's gaze landed on one of the desks that was now being used as a catchall for files, office supplies, past editions of the paper, and new packages of dog chew toys.

Moving to a smaller, cheaper office space outside of downtown Chatelaine had crossed his mind, but he wasn't ready to leave the good memories of being there with his father. Or Carly being there as well.

In his office, a tall, slender woman with brown hair dressed in casual clothes stood with her back toward him.

He walked in. "Morgana?"

She turned around. "Yes, hello."

At first glance, the young woman looked like a teenager, but her green eyes reflected a maturity that came with adulthood. He figured she was at least in her twenties.

Returning her smile, he shook her hand. "Nice to meet you, Morgana. I'm Devin. Have a seat."

She sat in front of the oak desk, and he settled into the chair behind it.

Just like his home, this office didn't have a lot of extras—just a desk, chairs, and a couple of filing cabinets and a couch along the wall.

But the space seemed a lot smaller without Chumley and all of the toys and other pet items Devin had bought to accommodate the large Great Dane. He'd given everything to Chumley's new owners, and they'd been grateful to have them.

Speaking of which…he'd received another message from the shelter. There was a strong chance that he would be fostering Francis until they found him a new home.

Out of habit, Devin flipped to a clean page in the spiral notebook in front of him. He always took notes during meetings and preferred the old-school way of writing things out when he was in his office. "So in your email, you mentioned you wanted to look through our archives. What time period are you interested in?"

Morgana adjusted the small backpack on her lap. "The mid-1960s through the early 1970s."

"Oh, you want to go *that* far back? We're still uploading the editions from those years into our system."

The young woman's gaze dropped as a look of disappointment came over her face. "So you can't help me."

"No—we can still help. It just might take a little time. Everything from those years is still stored on floppy disks."

Morgana perked up. "I don't mind searching through them. Can I start now?"

Her sudden shift to eagerness raised his curiosity. "I don't see why not." He stood. "Just let me check in with my staff assistant about the disks." Just before he reached the door, he paused. "Are you searching for anything in particular? It could help narrow the search for the files."

"No, but I'll know it when I see it." Morgana made steady eye contact with him, but she was clutching the backpack.

"Okay. Sit tight. I'll be back in a minute."

She exhaled with a smile. "Thanks."

He checked with Quinn. The disks were located in

the spare office where she'd been working on the filing project.

"All of the disks from 1960 to 1970 are in separate boxes," his assistant said. "I just took them out of storage, and I haven't gotten around to putting them in order, so she'll have to search them. There's also another box with disks that have labels with just headers but no dates. Did she mention what she was looking for? That box might be a place to start."

"She claims she doesn't know but that she'll recognize what it is when she sees it."

"Do you want me to help her sort through them?" Quinn offered.

Devin shook his head. It didn't make sense to pull her away from working on the paper with Charles, and he was curious to find out what Morgana was up to. He got the sense she was hiding something. "No, I'll do it."

A few minutes later, he stood in the spare office with the young woman. He opened a medium-sized box marked *1960* which he'd put on the desk. "Are you sure there isn't more to go on to help with your search?" he asked. "Like a year or a span of years or a particular subject, like birth or death announcements or real estate listings?" He was fishing for information, but it was worth a shot.

"I'm not looking for those types of records. I'm more interested in a time frame..." Frowning, she worried her lower lip with her teeth, almost as if she was afraid to say too much. "I should probably check out 1964 to 1965."

"That helps." He started taking disks out of the box and laying them on the desk. "Let's get to it."

"Oh, no—you're busy. I can do it."

"I don't mind. Things will go faster if you let me help

you weed through them. After that, I'll set you up on the computer with a disk reader and you can start your search."

She flashed him a grateful look. "That sounds good. Thank you."

"You're welcome."

Minutes ticked by as they sorted in silence.

As Devin added a disk to the 1964 stack, he asked, "Do you live in the area?"

"I guess you could say that." Morgana set aside a disk she didn't need. "I just moved here. I don't have a place yet, so I'm renting a room at the Chatelaine Motel."

It made sense that she was staying there. The motel functioned as an overnight lodging destination for travelers and a rooming house for extended visits. And it was the only option for anyone who didn't have friends or family in town.

"Well, if no one has told you yet, welcome to Chatelaine."

"Thanks." Her deliberate movements and her silence gave a clear message. She didn't want to talk about herself.

Devin set the question he really wanted to ask aside—why *had* she moved there? No one relocated to Chatelaine without a reason.

They finished sorting through the disks. He left Morgana to search through them and went back to the conference room.

A couple of hours later as he headed to his office, he glanced toward where Morgana worked. She was still at it. He should probably check and see how it was going. Just as he reached the threshold of the spare office, Morgana barreled out, almost running into him.

"Oh." She gave him a polite smile. "I was coming to

find you. I'm done. I wasn't sure what to do with the disks I was sorting through, so I left them on the desk."

"That's fine. Are you sure you won't be back? I can leave them out for you."

"No, but thanks for your help. I'm good."

But her expression reflected the opposite of good as she turned away. She looked kind of rattled.

Morgana left, and he went inside the spare office. As he went to put the disks back into the box, papers in the trash basket caught his eye.

He took them out and flattened them on the desk. From the way they were crumpled, they'd gotten caught in the printer.

Most of the main text was unreadable, but the headlines of the articles jumped out. *Worst Mining Disaster in History of Chatelaine... Bodies of 50 Victims Found in Silver Mine... Locals Demand Answers about the Mining Accident...*

She'd been researching the 1965 Fortune silver mine collapse? That seemed pretty specific considering Morgana had said she didn't know what she was looking for.

Devin slid the pile of disks she'd searched through closer to the computer and sat behind the desk. A stack of invoices waited for him in his office, but he would get to them later. Logically, the last disks she'd searched were on top.

Following Morgana's trail, he found the articles with the headlines on the crumpled pages and printed them out.

The articles had a few things in common. Their focus wasn't so much on the accident itself but the aftermath and speculation. And aside from Edgar and Elias Fortune, another name was prominent on the page. The mine foreman, Clint Wells, who'd also died in the collapse. They all seemed to point the blame to him.

Going with his instincts, Devin switched to searching for death announcements after the mining disaster and found one for Mr. Wells. He was survived by his wife Gwenyth and an eighteen-year-old daughter, Renee.

Devin sat back in the chair. Interesting.

The alarm on his phone chimed. *Carly...* She was at an after-school club meeting, and he was supposed to pick her up. If he was late, Lauren wouldn't hesitate to point that out during their first meeting with the mediator tomorrow morning.

He quickly put away the disks, shut down the computer, then hurried out the building to his truck.

All the while, his mind raced with thoughts of Morgana searching for information on the silver mine. Did she know something about those notes that had been left about there being a fifty-first miner who had perished? Or was her interest in the accident just a coincidence?

Chapter Eleven

Bea carried an order of Gulf shrimp and green-chili cheddar grits from the bustling kitchen into the dining room of the Cowgirl Café.

The clinking of glasses and silverware reverberated along with the murmur of conversations. And there were lots of satisfied smiles from the customers enjoying their meals.

She caught the eye of the blonde server who'd needed the order on-the-fly. The young woman had accidently keyed in the wrong item for one of her tables.

As the server rushed over to Bea, a look of relief was on her face. "Thank you."

"You're welcome." Bea gave her a reassuring smile.

Mistakes were bound to happen. But luckily nothing major, like stolen food, had occurred with tonight's rescheduled grand opening. The dining room was full, and although they hadn't experienced a huge rush as anticipated, business had been steady since they'd opened for dinner two hours ago. She was just grateful that so many people *had* decided to give her a second chance despite the comments online and the question about whether she deserved one.

I'm the newspaper's anonymous restaurant critic... I'm

sorry, Bea. You have every right to be angry with me. But as a restaurant critic, I couldn't show my bias no matter how I feel about you. This may be hard for you to believe right now, but my interest in you didn't just start the day of the wedding...

Devin's admission last week in the parking lot of the Saddle & Spur Roadhouse had floored her. And for some reason the content of the review had struck even harder knowing he was the source. Devin wasn't an anonymous stranger. He was someone she knew so intimately they were expecting a child together.

She'd received the results of the blood test yesterday from her doctor, confirming the pregnancy tests she'd taken and what she innately knew. But it still felt so surreal, especially since her first prenatal appointment wasn't for at least another six weeks. The biggest reminder that she was about to be a mom was the prenatal vitamins she'd started taking every day.

A server rushing through the dining room carrying empty plates briefly paused next to her. "Tanya needs you."

The next couple of hours were almost a blur as Bea moved from task to task, jumping in to expedite meals in the kitchen, clearing dirty dishes from tables in the dining room, and checking in with customers about their meals and the service.

Toward the front of the dining area, a dark-haired woman sitting by herself at a corner table drew her attention. She was trying to take bites from a biscuit in between soothing the fussy infant in her arms. Makeup adorned her face, but it didn't hide her harried expression. She finally gave up on eating and focused on the baby.

Bea wrestled with the vision of herself being in the

same situation. A sense of loneliness weighed down on her, mirroring what she'd felt that day buying the pregnancy test.

A tall, dark-haired guy walked into the restaurant carrying flowers. Spotting the woman with the baby, he hurried over to her.

Relief crossed the woman's face. He leaned down, and they shared a quick peck on the lips. Moments later, he sat across from her holding the baby. With the flowers lying beside her, the woman smiled as she dug into her salad.

Bea felt happy for her. The young mom wasn't alone. She had someone to share in the responsibility of caring for the child. And to support her as well. The man sitting with the baby might have been there for prenatal visits. The first ultrasound where they'd heard their child's heartbeat. Childbirth classes and the moment their child had entered the world.

At least that was what she imagined had happened for the couple. And possibly wanted for herself.

Devin had mentioned not wanting her to be alone or even feeling that she was on her own when it came to the baby—financially, emotionally, or on any other level.

It will be easier if you let me be there for you...

His words floated in her mind along with his apology and explanation for the critical review of her restaurant. He'd been honest with her. Wasn't that important? And now that the grand opening had occurred, did it even matter? Maybe it was time to set all that aside and focus on what was ahead.

Toward the end of the night, when business had slowed down, she slipped into her office and made a call.

He answered on the second ring. "Hello, Bea."

"Hi, Devin." Before she changed her mind, she pushed ahead. "Is there any chance we could talk tonight? I'm still at the restaurant, but I'll be free in an hour or so."

"Sure. Do you want me to come to you, or do you want to come here? I'm at home."

Once the restaurant closed, she wouldn't want to hang around. But meeting at her house could remind them of the awkwardness they'd experienced right after their perfect night together had gone sideways.

"I'll come to you."

Later on as she drove to his house outside Chatelaine, Bea practiced what she wanted to say to Devin.

"I would appreciate your help through the pregnancy. And of course I want you in our baby's life. But we should discuss the parameters, especially for the future."

A future that would include co-parenting their child for at least eighteen years.

But even after their child was on their own, she and Devin would be linked forever. Even if they weren't together.

She was attracted to Devin but rushing things along because of the baby would be a mistake. Sobering reality made Bea swallow hard. She'd pushed full speed ahead in marrying Jeff. Looking back, she'd deluded herself into believing she was taking a leap of faith. She'd convinced herself they were meant to be together while ignoring all the red flags that clearly indicated they shouldn't have.

After the divorce, she'd promised to never set up herself or anyone else for disappointment in a relationship by not facing facts. It had been easy to keep that promise since she hadn't found someone who'd piqued her interest in spending time with them. *Until Devin.* After their one night together, she'd started to think what more time with him might look like. Well, now she'd gotten that and then some—just not in the way she'd envisioned.

Bea parked in front of Devin's home. The stucco-and-brick ranch-style dwelling with a neatly trimmed lawn was similar to other houses on the street. At close to ten at night, the neighborhood was quiet.

As she stood at the front door, despite the dryness in her throat, she felt ready to embark on one of the most important conversations of her life. However, when the door opened, she couldn't speak.

Dressed in a burgundy T-shirt that clung to his muscular chest and a pair of black sweatpants, Devin was the perfect advertisement for casual, sexy, and relaxed. But as she looked into his eyes, she could see hints of apprehension.

"Hello." He stepped back and opened the door wider. "Come in."

"Thank you."

Their polite, stilted exchange felt out of place. Especially since the clean, freshly showered scent emanating from him as she walked inside made her want to throw herself into his arms and get up close and personal with him.

But she probably smelled like the café's entire menu—with an extra helping of Italian dressing courtesy of when a server had lost their grip on a salad they were carrying and accidently dumped most of it on her leg. She'd dabbed the stain, but the smell of vinegar and spices remained.

Devin shut the door behind her. "I was working in the living room. We can talk in there."

She followed him.

A light fixture with a ceiling fan illuminated the space.

Looking around, she noticed a crime drama playing on the television hanging on the wall across from a beige couch with camel-colored pillows that matched the side chairs.

Devin's laptop sat on the wood coffee table next to a plate with crumbs and a small pile of potato chips.

On the floor near the couch sat a new, plush-looking dog bed filled with packages of toys as well as harnesses and leashes.

"Excuse the mess. I bought a few things for the dog I'm fostering." He moved the pet supplies to the empty dining area.

"When are you picking him up?"

"This coming Saturday," he replied.

As she sat in one of the side chairs, the story he'd told her about Chumley came to mind. "Is it another Great Dane?"

"No. It's a terrier mix this time. His owner is moving to a senior-living apartment and can't take the dog with him."

"Oh no! That's so sad."

"It is. But the shelter is really successful in finding pets new homes."

"That's good." As Devin stood by the couch, she met his gaze. The speech she'd practiced felt like an awkward lead-in to the next topic of conversation. But what *should* they talk about?

As the pause stretched on, she looked away from him and her gaze landed on the plate of chips. The Cobb salad she'd nibbled on around noon was a distant memory. She'd tasted a few of the entrées before dinner service, but that had been only a few bites and not a complete meal.

Her stomach gurgled.

If she were sitting on the couch, she might have snagged a few chips to stave off hunger.

Devin picked up the plate. “Can I get you anything?”

Her stomach answered with a full-on growl.

He arched a brow. “When did you last eat?”

The way he pinned her with his dark brown gaze was like a dose of truth serum. “I tasted a few of the entrées with Tanya before dinner.”

“Turkey or ham?”

“We don’t serve turkey on the menu…and that’s not what you’re talking about.”

“No. I’m going to make you a grilled sandwich, and I was wondering which one you wanted. Or you can have both.”

A hint of amusement came into his eyes and a faint smile shadowed his mouth. A recollection of the many kisses they’d shared—luxuriously long, intensely passionate, spicy yet sweet—passed through her mind.

Her mouth started to water. Could she have a sandwich *and* a smooch on the side? “Turkey would be great.”

“What about cheese? I have cheddar or Swiss.”

“Swiss, please, and a little mustard.” Did that request sound like a demand? He wasn’t running a restaurant. “Actually, I don’t mind doing it. Just point the way.”

She moved to stand, but he waved her off. “No. You’ve been running around all night. Relax… I’ve got this.”

He left, and a short time later, she heard sounds echoing from the kitchen.

It was strange having a guy wait on her like this.

Restlessness almost brought Bea to her feet. She occupied the time by taking advantage of the moment to see what the simple furnished space told her about Devin.

Aside from the laptop and dog paraphernalia, the only other things that gave a peek into his life was a small stack of mail on the coffee table and framed photos of him with Carly at various ages on the media console.

Devin returned carrying a plate with the sandwich cut in half with chips on the side. He was also holding a glass of lemonade. He handed her the food, then snagged a piece of junk mail to put under the glass on the coffee table.

"Thank you. But I don't think I can eat all of this." She took a bite of the heated sandwich, and a grateful moan slipped out. "This is so good."

"You're welcome. Sit back and enjoy it. Don't worry about leftovers." He sat down and started watching television.

Bea took several more bites before remembering why she was there. But fortunately, she didn't feel self-conscious at all not talking and just eating. The awkwardness she'd felt earlier had transformed into a comfortable silence.

He looked relaxed as well. The space on the couch next to him looked like the perfect spot to be. It was too easy to imagine herself there with her shoes off and her feet curled underneath her as she rested her head on his shoulder.

Suddenly, she felt lonely in the side chair.

After finishing almost three-quarters of the sandwich and all the chips, she put the plate on the table and picked up the glass of lemonade. It was just the right combination of cold, tart, and sweet.

Devin glanced over at her. "Better?"

"Yes. And you don't have to say it."

"Say what?" he asked lightly.

"That I have to do a better job of taking care of myself…now that I'm pregnant."

"You should take care of yourself in general, but yes,

now that you're pregnant, skipping meals isn't a good idea."

"I know." She sighed. "Today was just so busy. Now that the grand opening is over, I can focus on other things."

"Did everything go well tonight?"

"It did. We had a full house. And everyone seemed pleased with the food." Curiosity made her ask. "So will my restaurant receive a review?"

"It will. But not by me, of course. I'm more than a little biased about the owner. So aside from a little hungry, how are you feeling?"

"Correction—I *was* hungry. But honestly, I don't feel any different than I did a few weeks ago. But that will change." It was time to stop stalling and get to why she was there. Bea put the glass on the table. "Thank you for giving me time to think about everything. Of course I want you to be in our baby's life, but like I said before, I don't want you to feel pressured to be there."

"I don't." Devin rose from the couch. After moving the plate and the glass with the junk mail aside, he sat on the coffee table in front of her. "And like I said before, I don't want to just know my child. I would like to get to know you as well. I like you a lot, Bea. And I think you like me, too. Or am I wrong…?"

Denying she still wanted to jump him in a very good way wouldn't get her anywhere. "No, you're not wrong. But attraction doesn't make a relationship."

"But it's a start. I know you and I had agreed to one night together, but I can't lie. My plan had been to ask if you would consider going out with me again once things settled down for you. And yes, I would have confessed that I was the restaurant critic." He took hold of her hand. "All

I would have wanted then and still want now is a chance for us to get to know each other."

The guy she'd been crushing on like a schoolgirl for months wanted a chance with her. It was like a moment out of romance movie. But this wasn't a scripted scene. This was *real life*...and there was a baby to think about.

She met his gaze. "We have to take it slow. No rushing into anything. And if it doesn't work for us to be together, we have to be ready to accept that."

"I agree with all of that, but I have a question."

"What?" she asked a bit anxiously.

"Does taking it slow include holding you?"

"Yes." His huge grin eased her nerves and made her smile. "What are you smiling so big about?"

He tugged her to her feet and led her to the couch. "I'm happy you didn't hesitate in answering me."

As soon as they sat down, Bea did what she'd longed to do. She kicked off her shoes and curled up next to him.

His chest rose and fell under her palm with a deep breath. "This is better."

"It is." She hadn't realized how badly she'd needed to be held. Bea laid her head on his shoulder. "So, we've agreed to get to know each other. What happens next?"

Chapter Twelve

Devin loaded the pet carrier and leash into the back seat of his truck parked in front of his house. He'd spend the morning proofreading the final version of the newspaper before sending it to the printer. After that, he would pick up Bea at the restaurant around noon for their first date. They were going to the pet shelter to get Francis.

The first few days with a rescue animal were critical. Francis was probably missing his owner. The pup might want extra attention, or he could be withdrawn. All Devin could do was try to make Francis comfortable and convey that he was there for him. Given time, the dog would come to realize he was safe.

That sense of being there and safety was what he wanted Bea to feel in their relationship as well.

The one thing that was clear—chemistry existed between them. It had been there from the start. That part of their connection had led them to their one night together, but Bea becoming pregnant could lead to a relationship that went beyond co-parenting. Exploring that possibility didn't feel like rushing to him but a natural next step. But he had to respect that Bea felt differently.

When she'd mentioned that she hadn't been able to conceive eight years ago, he'd sensed that she hadn't received support or maybe even compassion from her now ex-husband. It was understandable that she might want to keep her guard up and not risk getting hurt again.

Done packing up pet supplies, Devin got behind the wheel, started the engine, and headed for work. Traffic leading out of the neighborhood was sluggish, and a few miles down the road he found out why. Construction was happening, and there was a detour before the main road.

Following the directions of the worker managing traffic, he turned left.

Looks like I'm taking the scenic route... Devin settled in for a longer ride to town.

Homes sat back from the side of the road. Every now and then, he passed a ranch and open pastures with cows or horses.

He didn't travel this way often, but he recognized the area. He was just a few miles from Fortune's Castle.

The detour ended.

Turning right would lead him back to the four-lane road that would take him to town. But if he went left…

Giving in to the impulse, Devin made a left turn. A short time later, he turned right onto a long tree-lined private driveway. Up ahead, a security gate stretched across the narrow road sat open, and he drove past through it. Yards away in the distance sat Fortune's Castle.

A short time later, he walked up the cobblestone pathway toward the replica of a medieval castle. The decades-old concrete structure boasted so many features, it was hard to decide what to focus on first—ornate pointed arches, flying buttresses, gargoyles, or the stained-glass windows.

He'd been there once with his father when he'd been a

boy. Carl had been covering a special event. The grounds had been open to the public but not the castle.

Devin reached the large wooden door. A speaker was built into the wall on the left, but there wasn't an intercom button. He used the ornate knocker shaped like a lion's head in the middle of the door.

Wendell refusing to speak with him was the worst that could happen. Other than that, Devin had nothing to lose.

The older man's voice came through the speaker. "Hello?"

"Hello, Wendell. It's Devin from the *Chatelaine Daily News*."

"Who?"

He spotted a camera up high and off the side and looked straight into it. "It's Devin Street. We've met before. I own the local newspaper."

"I know who you are. What do you want?"

"I'm hoping you can clear up some new information I came across about the silver mine accident." Wanting to get Wendell's attention, he added, "There's a young woman in town looking into it as well. Maybe you know her?"

A click echoed from the door as Wendell answered through the speaker. "Come in."

Devin opened the door and walked into a grand entryway with black-and-white checkerboard floor tiles. An elaborate wrought-iron candelabra hung from the ceiling painted with a Byzantine-style mosaic of peacocks and birds.

Black torch-shaped sconces interspersed with paintings of medieval lords and ladies in outdoor landscapes lined the left side of the wall along with abbey bench seats.

A sweeping ruby-colored carpeted staircase led up to the landing of the second floor.

Whoa... The rumors were right. The castle was strange and oddly magnificent at the same time.

Devin walked to the middle of the entryway and stood by a round glass table. The base of it was three knights in coats of armor holding swords and shields while on bended knee.

From what he'd heard, there were a lot of references to the number fifty cleverly embedded in the paintings and the artwork. And trying to find them was equivalent to a scavenger hunt. That wasn't surprising considering how the older generations of the Fortune family were all a big mystery.

"Wendell?" he called out.

A door on the right framed by an arch opened.

Wendell stood in the doorway. "I'm here."

The older man's bushy gray beard almost swallowed his gaunt face. A gray cardigan, white button-down and jeans hung loosely on this thin frame.

Devin walked to Wendell. "Thanks for taking a minute to talk to me this morning."

As they shook hands, Wendell's grip was weak and his hand felt cold and frail. Weariness shadowed his blue eyes. "You drove all the way out here. You must have something important to ask."

Important? Wendell clearly wasn't well. Maybe Devin shouldn't have disturbed him. A hint of regret pinged inside of him as he followed the older man inside the room.

"Have a seat." Wendell shuffled across the black-and-silver rug and dropped into the leather chair behind a large, polished wood desk. Behind him, floor-to-ceiling shelves with books filled the entire wall.

Devin sat in the red upholstered chair across from him.

He pulled up the Notes app on his phone. "The questions I have won't take up too much of your time. I've been looking through a series of articles written by the paper about the mining accident. One name keeps popping up—Clint Wells."

"That's not surprising." Wendell's face remained neutral as he settled himself in the chair. "He was the foreman."

"Yes. And he had a wife, Gwenyth, and an eighteen-year-old daughter, Renee. Do you remember what happened to them?"

"They left town soon after the accident. I don't know where they went, and it's been my understanding that no one's heard from them since."

"Clint was initially blamed for the accident. Did anyone attempt to let them know other parties may have been involved and that he possibly wasn't to blame?"

Wendell's eyes briefly narrowed as he cleared his throat. "By *other parties*, you mean my brothers, Edgar and Elias."

"Yes. The accusations were damning and most likely led to them leaving town."

"As far as I know, no one reached out to them with that information. And it might not have made a difference to them. Clint was gone along with the other forty-nine miners."

"Or possibly fifty-one miners, like the notes have claimed?"

Agitated, Wendell waved him off. "Clint's widow is in her eighties now, and their daughter is in her fifties. I'm sure they would just like to continue to go on with their lives. No one wants to remember that terrible time."

"Respectfully, I have to disagree. The person who wrote the notes does. And a young woman spent most of an afternoon in my office looking up this information."

"A young woman? Who?" Wendell demanded.

"Her name is Morgana. She's new to the area."

"I don't know who she is. And I don't have the answer to your questions."

The old man's implacable expression signaled the meeting was over.

Devin stood. "Well, I appreciate your time. And if you do remember something, I hope you'll reach out to me so we can get the real story on record and end the speculation."

Wendell opened his mouth as if to say something but paused. "I'll keep that in mind. Forgive me for not walking you to the door. I'm a little tired."

"Not at all. I'll show myself out." Devin went to the office door. Before he walked out he looked back.

Wendell was staring at a series of black-and-white photographs in silver frames hanging on the side wall. As he rested a hand on his forehead, he sank wearily back in his seat.

Later that afternoon, Devin was on the road with Bea headed to the Chatelaine Veterinary Clinic, where the pet shelter was located.

She looked casual and cute in jeans, a peach-colored sweatshirt, and tennis shoes.

They were just outside of town. Traffic on the four-lane road started to thin out as cars pulled into the parking lot of the Saddle & Spur Roadhouse and, farther up, GreatStore.

Devin glanced over at Bea. She hadn't said much since he'd picked her up. Last night, she'd told him things were going well at the restaurant. Had that changed?

Settling in for the half-hour ride, he set the cruise control for a little higher than the speed limit. Visiting Fortune's Castle had put him behind schedule. "Thanks for coming with me this afternoon. I know you're busy. Now that the opening is over, how are things going?"

"Good." A distracted expression was on her face as she smiled. "What about you?"

"The usual. The paper is with the printer now, and we're not anticipating any major distribution issues tomorrow. And I'm working on stories for the next edition." He cleared his throat, then went on to say, "Oh, and I went to see your uncle today. I wanted to talk to him about the foreman who'd worked at the Fortunes' silver mine when the accident happened."

"That was nice." Bea tucked a strand of hair behind her ear and looked out the window.

Nice? Had she even heard him? "Space creatures from Venus were involved."

"Venus?" She looked at him. "What are you talking about?"

"Just checking to see if you were with me. You seemed preoccupied about something."

"I am…just a little." She sighed. "Okay, maybe more than a little. I came across an article online with information for expectant moms, and I kind of fell down a rabbit hole."

"I'm guessing it was a deep one?"

"Yes. There were all these lists." She grimaced. "Actually they were lists within a list within another list."

He furrowed a brow. "What do you mean?"

"For instance, on the newborn-essentials checklist, there's baby gear, and all the stuff needed for feeding, and diapering. And then there were suggestions from real moms about what to do and what not to do. The diapering issue…wow. I didn't know there was such a huge debate about cloth or disposable. I usually like lists, but this was…intimidating."

The days of parental judgment and guilt in figuring out what to do with a newborn…he remembered them well. It wasn't surprising Bea was feeling overwhelmed. "From my experience, while lists can be helpful, everyone's childcare experiences are different. You'll find ways and hacks for circumstances that work for you."

Bea gave him a skeptical look. "Including diapering hacks?"

"As strange as that may sound, yes. I still remember a few. Things like using a practical onesie versus those ones with all the snaps and buttons. When you're changing lots of diapers—trust me, simple is the way to go. And having an emergency diaper stash in almost every room and the car is a must."

She laughed. "It sounds like you're remembering just fine."

"I'm sure more will come back to me. But at the same time, after thirteen years, I'm sure some of the practices have changed."

"I thought sorting through food recipes to find the right one was stressful." Bea worried her lower lip, then sighed. "There's just so much to take in."

Devin reached out and laid his hand over Bea's resting on her thigh. "But you don't have to take it in all at once. The key is don't be afraid to ask, especially when you need something from me."

"You're right," she replied softly.

Most of the apprehension left Bea's face, but from the look in her eyes, something was still on her mind.

Chapter Thirteen

As Devin gave her hand a squeeze, she conjured up a smile, but she couldn't entirely let go of the anxiety hovering inside of her.

The lists in general were overwhelming, but one in particular remained on her mind—the parenting questionnaire.

Homebase for the baby. Prearranging a childcare schedule. Health insurance. There were so many things she and Devin needed to discuss before the baby arrived. He was right about not having to do everything right away. But even so, she needed to know where his responsibilities would begin and end.

"If I sent you the lists, would you take a look at them? And there's a parenting questionnaire, too."

"Of course I will. Email them to me."

Bea released an easy breath. Her ex would have given her a thousand and one reasons why he couldn't read them.

"We're here." Devin pointed to a long white building with green trim surrounded by open land.

There was a simplicity to the place, and it had a sanctuary vibe.

"It's a veterinarian clinic," he added. "And it also has

a pet spa, and they provide space for the fostering and adoption service."

He pulled in and parked.

They got out, and Bea preceded him down the sidewalk to the entrance.

Inside the building, in the tidy reception area with orange seating along the wall, owners and their pets waited to see the vet.

The receptionist at the front desk greeted them.

"Hello," Devin replied. "I'm here to pick up a dog I'm fostering for the shelter. My name is Devin Street."

The woman checked her computer screen. "Yes, they're expecting you. One of the volunteers will meet you in the play area. Do you know where that is?"

"I do. Thanks." Devin led the way down an adjoining hallway.

They exited at the end into an outdoor space with colorful ramps and slides in various configurations arranged on fake turf.

A teenage boy was cleaning up a square patch of real grass off to the side. From the scowl on his face, he was the very definition of boredom and unhappiness.

Chuckling, Devin murmured, "Guess his day isn't going well."

"Give him a break. Would you be smiling if you were spending a sunny Saturday picking up dog poop?"

"It's a character-building experience." He shrugged. "When I was his age, I spent a lot of weekends doing things that weren't fun."

"Like what?" Bea asked.

"I washed my dad's car. Mowed the lawn, and it wasn't a tiny patch like that one. It was a couple of acres. And

I also folded most of the newspapers for Sunday's home delivery, and I even had my own paper route."

"You *were* busy." It wasn't surprising to hear that even growing up Devin had had a full schedule.

"Looking back, I guess I was—partly because I was an only child and didn't have a sibling to share the load. But mostly because my dad wanted to keep me out of trouble."

"You caused trouble?" She feigned shock. "No, I don't believe that."

He laughed. "Wait a minute. You have doubts? Okay, what about you? Did you have chores growing up, or did you just play all day?"

"*Play all day?* I wish. I rotated through chores along with Esme and Asa. Laundry, mowing the lawn, taking out the garbage."

"What about cooking? Did you guys help out with that, too?"

"Asa and Esme, not so much. But I didn't mind. Helping my mom in the kitchen was our special time together. While we cooked, I could really talk to her about things." A twinge of nostalgia hit Bea. Her mom had always had the answers, even when it had come to the most challenging things. What she wouldn't give to hear her mom's advice now that she was an expectant mother-to-be.

A couple of tears leaked from her eyes. Bea was shocked to feel them on her cheeks. Were pregnancy hormones kicking in this soon?

Looking down, she quickly batted them away. "Sorry—I don't know why I'm crying."

"Because you miss her." Devin traced a tear from her cheek. "And that's okay. I miss my dad, too."

"Our child won't have grandparents..." The realization made her a bit sadder.

"But they'll have plenty of aunts and uncles—and cousins on your side of the family. And Carly as an older sister." He cupped her cheek. "And they'll have us."

The warmth of his touch enveloped her. It was so natural to move closer and lean into his one-arm embrace.

An older woman with black-and-silver hair styled in a casual updo walked out the door. A high school–aged girl followed her, leading a Jack Russell–cocker spaniel, mixed-breed dog on a leash. They both wore short blue aprons over their clothes featuring the name of the shelter.

The woman strode toward them. "Hi—you must be Devin. I'm Meg."

"Yes, hello." Devin shook hands with her. "Meg, this is Bea." As he turned toward Bea, he gently laid a hand on her back.

She returned the woman's smile. "Hello."

Meg looked to the teen and the small brown-and-white dog who was off the leash and sniffing near a bench. "This is Emma, one of our student volunteers, and that's Francis. He's three years old. As you know, his owner couldn't care for him any longer. He dropped him off a little over a week ago. I actually thought we had an adoption lined up for the pup yesterday, but it fell through. I'm so glad you can take him in."

"I'm happy to help," Devin said. "How's he been adjusting through the change?"

"As expected, he was withdrawn at first, but he's interacting with everyone more now. We think he'll do much better in a home setting. While you two get acquainted with him, I'll get his things. He has a dog bed he's partial to, and we're going to give you a bag of what we've been feeding him. Oh, and you'll need this." She took a worn-looking yellow ball from the pocket of her apron and handed it to Bea. "This is his favorite toy. Maybe he'll play with you a bit. It might help him feel more comfortable in leaving with you."

As Bea turned to give the ball to Devin, Francis shyly approached, eyeing the toy. He lay down a few feet away and dropped his head onto his front paws.

Devin held up his hands, refusing the toy. "I think Francis wants his possession back."

Unsure of what to do, she shrugged. "Do I just throw it?"

"No. Lay it on the ground. Let's see if he'll come to us to get it."

"Hi, Francis. Do you want your ball?" Bea leaned over, and as she set the ball down, the pup lifted his head. "Now what?"

"We talk to each other. Direct eye contact can be perceived as threatening to a dog, especially if he doesn't know you."

Bea turned to Devin. "So we just stand here?"

"For a little bit."

She chuckled. "This feels like an audition."

"Relax. You're doing fine," he assured her.

The wind blew a strand of hair near her eyes.

Devin reached up and smoothed it back behind her ear. As his hand lingered, his gaze dropped to her lips.

Bea's heart skipped several beats. Despite wanting to, she still hadn't kissed him yet. Memories of how their lip-locks had ignited like sparks to flame their one night together played through her mind. Kissing him would probably make taking things slow a really torturous experience.

He glanced to the side. "Looks like we have a visitor."

Francis stood at Bea's feet. His liquid brown eyes tugged at her heartstrings, and she offered him her hand. He sniffed it. His tail wagged a little, and she kept petting him.

Devin greeted Francis, and they both interacted with him. After a while, the pup became more comfortable, and when Bea lobbed the ball a short distance away, he returned it.

"I think he's ready to go now." Devin went to get the crate.

Bea scratched Francis behind his ears and cooed, "You're going to a nice safe place, and we're going to take good care of you." Wait. No, not *we*—Devin.

Meg walked over to Bea. "I can tell Francis is going to be in good hands." She beamed a friendly smile. "Once he gets used to his surroundings, he'll be a charmer. And he's definitely baby-tester material for the right couple."

Baby? Bea barely stopped herself from laying a hand on her abdomen. But there was no way this woman could know that she was pregnant.

"I'm sorry." Meg's smile sobered a little. "My little joke didn't go over well. Sometimes couples adopt a fur baby in preparation for a real one."

"Oh, but we're not..." Bea stumbled over what to say. She and Devin weren't a couple, but they were expecting.

He returned with the carrier. "Okay, Francis, let's go for a ride."

Once the dog was settled, they were ready to leave. After saying goodbye to Meg, they retraced their steps down the hall, through the reception area and out the door.

They secured the carrier with Francis on the back seat.

As Devin shut the back passenger side door, he smiled at Bea standing beside the truck. "Thanks again for coming. You made the transition a whole lot easier for him."

"I'm glad I could help. It gives me hope." She laughed. "If I can handle a dog, then maybe I can handle a baby."

"You can. You're compassionate. You care. You're going to be a great mom, Bea."

The assurance in his eyes almost erased her doubts. "You really think so?"

He lightly grasped her shoulders. "I do."

Bea laid her hands on his chest. Devin was so solid and real with his intentions. It was hard not to lean on him.

As she moved closer, he glided his hands toward her back.

"Um…excuse me." Emma stood nearby, holding up a leash. She looked between the two of them with a curious, slightly judgy expression. "This belongs to Francis. He's used to using it. Meg said you should take it with you."

"Thanks." As Devin accepted the leash, Bea got into the truck.

He went around to the other side. After settling into the driver's seat, he put his phone in the open section of the center console.

Bea remained baffled by the girl. "Did you see the way she looked at us? I feel like I'm her age again and just got caught making out with my boyfriend."

"Teens are like that when it comes to PDA. Carly's the same way."

"So what will you tell her about us?" she asked.

"That depends on you. Do you want to wait a while before officially telling everyone about the baby?"

She pursed her lips, contemplating. "Maybe we *should* wait. It's still early."

"Okay, we wait." Devin turned to look at her. "And what about us? Are we telling people that we're seeing each other?"

"I guess there's no point in hiding it. In fact, I think it would be impossible."

He quirked a brow. "Why's that?"

"Because when we're together, we're not exactly keeping our hands off of each other."

"We're not?" He reached over and took her hand, intertwining their fingers.

She laughed.

He angled more toward her. "But I'm confused. Why is not being able to keep our hands off of each other a bad thing?"

From the look in Devin's eyes, he was far from confused, but Bea played along. "Because touching leads to kissing."

"That's just a theory."

"No, it's a fact." Giving in to what she'd wanted to do since last night, Bea leaned in and pressed her mouth to his.

As Devin cupped her cheek, she parted her lips and the kiss deepened.

Just as she'd suspected, the simmering embers of desire from their first night hadn't completely died away. A part of her crossed her fingers and toes, hoping their connection would only grow stronger. But practicality needled that hope. They would also face trials along the way.

The rattling of his phone buzzing in the console broke into the moment, and they eased out of the kiss.

Devin grabbed his phone, and as he checked the screen

his expression sobered. “Damn,” he whispered. “She already knows.”

“She?” Bea glanced at his phone, then him. “You mean your ex-wife?”

Devin’s jaw angled as another text came in. “No… Carly.”

Chapter Fourteen

"So it's true?" Lauren's voice rose an octave. "What happened to our agreement about letting the other know about major changes in our lives?"

Devin took several steps toward the cluster of bushes on the back wall behind Lauren's house. She followed him.

They were yards past the deck and screened-in pool, but the window in Carly's room upstairs faced the backyard. She'd been in her room since hearing about Bea and the baby. And, not surprisingly, she was upset about what she'd found out.

Michaela and the damn pizza oven had struck again. Carly had been over at her friend's house when Michaela's older sister, Emma, had spilled the news. The same Emma who'd brought Francis to the outdoor play area and delivered the leash to him and Bea at the truck. She'd witnessed them together and overheard them talking about the baby.

Devin modulated his voice. "I didn't intentionally break our agreement. My relationship with Bea happened recently."

"And the two of you decided to have a baby already."

During the subsequent pause, as Lauren looked at his face, her eyes widened. "It wasn't planned? Well, that's definitely going to spice up the next birds-and-bees conversation I have with Carly. The good thing is you probably made the conversation about telling her she's moving to Corpus Christi a lot easier."

"Moving?" He worked to control his tone. "That's something we're still discussing with the mediator on Monday."

"Seriously? The main reason our marriage ended was because our relationship fell second or third to everything else. Do you really think you can balance having a baby, being the primary co-parent of our daughter, *and* running the newspaper?"

The main reason? Devin struggled to get past Lauren's claim about what had caused their marriage to collapse. They'd grown apart. At least that was how he saw it. But debating their points of view on why they'd divorced wouldn't change anything.

"I can't undo the past. But I can and will build a future that includes Carly, Bea, and the child she and I are having together."

As Lauren shook her head, exasperation filled her face. She opened her mouth to speak, then she shut it. "There's no point in discussing it now." She pointed to the house. "What are you going to tell our daughter?"

"The truth."

"If telling her the truth doesn't work, you're about to have an interesting week," Lauren told him. "I have to go to Corpus Christi for a meeting. I leave on Tuesday, and she's all yours until after her event on Saturday."

"What event?" he asked.

"The school fundraiser. I sent you the text the other day."

"Right. I'll handle it." Somehow he'd missed it. He'd search through his messages when he got home. But first he needed to straighten things out with his daughter.

Moments later, Devin sat with Carly at the patio table on the deck. Her arms were crossed over her chest. The stubborn look on her face as she stared out at the pool reminded him of Lauren.

"I'm sorry you found out about Bea and the baby this way," he said quietly. "We'd planned on telling you, your mom, and everyone else. We just wanted to wait a few more weeks."

Carly looked at him. Hurt shadowed the accusation in her eyes. "So you're getting married?"

He and Lauren had agreed it was important to tell the truth about his relationship with Bea. But they'd decided to still wait a while longer to tell Carly about Lauren's new job and working out a new custody agreement.

Devin rested his arms on the table. "Bea and I haven't discussed that. But we are committed to raising the baby." He leaned forward. "But none of that changes how I feel about you. I love you, Carly, and you are and will always be my daughter."

"But she'll be, like, my *stepmother*, won't she?" Carly hadn't put *wicked* in front of *stepmother*, but her tone more than implied it.

Of course, he hoped that Bea and Carly would grow closer. Having someone like Bea to turn to as well as him and Lauren could be a bonus for the teen. But he couldn't speak for Bea.

"The type of relationship you and Bea will have is something that will develop over time. My only hope is that when you meet Bea, you'll give her a chance."

"Are you sure inviting me to dinner was a good idea?" Bea straightened the placemats on the square table in

Devin's kitchen for the second time. "Maybe we should have waited a few more weeks."

He removed silverware from a drawer then walked over to her. "I'm sure. You being here tonight *is* a good idea. Trust me."

Still, Bea couldn't shake off a feeling of doubt as he laid out the forks, knives and spoons.

Carly had just left to walk Francis a few minutes before she had arrived. If she left now, Devin could claim an emergency had happened at the restaurant and she'd had to leave.

Bea sunk her teeth into her lower lip, holding back on suggesting that to Devin. No. She'd agreed to join him and Carly for dinner, and she was going to see it through.

Schedule wise it worked out. It was Tuesday night, and things were slow at the café. Maybe that was a sign that she *should* be there. But realistically, they couldn't forget Carly had just found out about them that past Saturday. And that she had not only been upset about the news, but also how she'd heard about the situation.

Yesterday, Emma's mother had contacted her, apologizing for her daughter's behavior. She'd also said that if the teen or her younger sister Michaela repeated the news, by the time they got their phones back, the technology would be so obsolete they wouldn't remember how to use them.

Ouch. Bea almost felt sorry for the girls when their mom had mentioned that level of a restriction.

Devin turned Bea by the waist to face him. "I know you're anxious. And I have to admit, I'm a little nervous, too. But there's no point in holding this off. But when I asked Carly about you joining us for dinner, she was okay with it."

Bea glimpsed a hint of reservation in his eyes. "Is that really what she said?"

"No, she said, 'Whatever,' but in teen speak, that's as good as a yes. And honestly, I think that's the best answer we're going to get from her for now." He gave Bea a light squeeze. "She's not going to accept us overnight, but this is a start. And she has an event coming up that I told her you might be able to give her some advice on."

"What is it?"

"Nothing big. For extra credit in one of her classes, as a group, they had to organize a fundraiser. They're having a bake sale on Saturday. The proceeds will go to nonprofits in the area like the pet shelter and the Chatelaine Fish and Wildlife Conservation Society. She's not sure what to make. Talking about it with her could help break the ice."

"I hope so." Bea laid her hands on his chest. "The last thing I want is to come between you and your daughter. Or for our relationship to impact the custody agreement you're trying to work out with Lauren. You never told me how the meeting with the mediator went the other day."

He gave her a lopsided smile. "Well, Lauren and I definitely aired our grievances. But the mediator made valid points. Despite our differences, we both love our daughter and that has to be the guiding factor. He suggested we each draw up a day-to-day schedule as the primary co-parent. It would allow us to understand what the other wants and expects for Carly's care."

"So how do you see it working?"

"Well, when it comes to school, I don't see much changing, except for I'll be the one dropping her off. After school, she normally takes the bus home. When extracurricular activities happen, we usually carpool with other parents. Day-to-day expectations and responsibilities won't change either."

Curious, Bea asked, "When will she see her mom?"

He released a breath. "From my point of view, I'm thinking two weekends a month and designated holidays. Which ones, I would like to leave that choice to Lauren and Carly."

And what about her and the baby? Concern rose in Bea that he hadn't mentioned them in the plan. But surely, he was including them.

The front door opened.

"Dad!" Carly called out. "The food is here."

"Coming." Devin pressed a kiss near Bea's ear and whispered, "It's going to work. We've got this." He snagged the tip from the counter for the delivery person and went to meet them.

Jitters swirled in Bea stomach. *We've got this.* That meant he was thinking of them as a team, right? Maybe she was reading too much into what he hadn't said. It didn't mean he wasn't factoring her and the baby into the ultimate plan.

A moment later, Devin came back into the kitchen with the food. He set the bag on the counter. "Carly's washing her hands. She'll be here in a minute. I forgot to ask what you liked, so I got a variety. Fried rice, lo mein, egg rolls, and three different entrées. Hope you're hungry."

"I am." She'd had a full day and only eaten a muffin for breakfast and a salad for lunch. But she wasn't confessing that to Devin.

As he started putting containers on the counter, Bea caught a whiff of garlic. Usually, the pungent aroma raised anticipation for flavorful food, but the smell was like an assault on her senses. Had something gone bad?

Devin opened one of the boxes, and the smell grew stronger. “Mmm. Chicken in garlic sauce. Just the smell of this is making me extra hungry.”

She surreptitiously covered her nose with her fingers and stepped back.

Carly walked into the kitchen.

Smiling, Devin placed his hand lightly on Bea’s arm. “This is my daughter, Carly.”

Bea could see Carly’s resemblance to Devin. She had his eyes and maybe his smile if she would have given a genuine one instead of what came with her slightly tart expression.

“Hello.” Carly went to the refrigerator.

Devin spoke to Carly, “While you’re in there, grab the iced tea.” He gave Bea a reassuring glance as he gave her hand a brief squeeze.

They worked together bringing the food, drinks, and plates to the table, then sat down.

Devin nudged the container of chicken in garlic sauce toward Bea. “Carly and I have been known to fight over this, but as our guest, we’ll give you first dibs.”

“Oh, no—that’s okay…”

Bea held her breath and quickly passed the container to Carly seated next to her. But the smell seemed to linger and her appetite started to wane. She put a little fried rice on her plate along with an egg roll.

Carly put some chicken and garlic sauce on her plate, then set the container between them. “You don’t like the food?”

“No, it’s great.” Bea moved the container toward the middle of the table.

As Devin glanced at the small portion of food on her

plate, she saw questions in his eyes. Earlier she'd told him she was hungry.

"So how are things at the café?" he asked.

Thankful for the change of topic, she told him briefly about the anniversary party they were catering.

"I'm sure the kids will enjoy the ice cream sundae bar," he said. "Too bad you can't do something like that at the fundraiser this weekend, Carly."

"It's a bake sale." Carly picked up the container of chicken and garlic. She added some to her plate, then plopped the container right next to Bea.

It tipped over, and some of the contents spilled out.

Bea's stomach roiled. If she didn't leave right now, she'd hurl. She stood. "Excuse me."

As she hurried from the kitchen and into the dining room, the sliding glass door with the view of the wide-open backyard caught her attention. Bea opened it, walked out on the deck, and sucked in fresh air.

Feeling a little shaky, she sat down on the porch swing. She'd never had that reaction to food before. How embarrassing.

Devin walked out onto the porch carrying a mug. "Are you all right?"

"Yes—I was just feeling a bit closed in." As he offered her the mug, she looked up at him. "What is it?"

"Ginger-and-lemon tea. I didn't put any sweetener in it. I have sugar or honey."

Bea inhaled the steam, then took a sip. The warmth of the beverage soothed her stomach. "This is perfect."

He sat beside her, and the swing rocked a little. "Why didn't you tell me the food didn't agree with you?"

"It wasn't all the food. Just the smell of the garlic in the sauce. You mentioned it was your and Carly's favorite. I didn't want to deprive you of it."

"You're pregnant, Bea. If certain tastes or smells get to you, you're allowed to speak up, especially to me." He laid his arm behind her on the swing.

"If this is the precursor to morning sickness, I think I'm in trouble." Following his lead, she rested her head on his shoulder.

"Hopefully the tea will help."

"Is there one that will help me give birth and learn how to be a parent? When the baby's here, I won't be able to cop out when I don't feel well." Reality broke through, and anxiety started to replace Bea's lightheartedness. "I'll be responsible for a small person who will depend on me for everything, but they won't be able to tell me what they need, and I'll probably get it wrong. And then they'll grow into a bigger person who will be able to tell me what they want, but I'll probably still get it wrong."

"You're getting way ahead of yourself." Devin kissed her temple. "Yes, parenting can be scary, and sure, sometimes kids are hard to figure out, but there will be good moments, too. And whatever comes our way, we'll go through the experience together. Okay?"

Bea looked at his face. Seeing the confidence in his dark brown eyes made it easy to believe him.

"Okay." She settled her head back onto his shoulder.

His solid strength, the tea, the sway of the swing. The bright hues of yellow and orange surrounding the setting sun. As Bea soaked it all in, she started to feel better… and her eyelids grew heavy.

Devin slipped the cup from her hand. "Do you want to

stay the night? You can sleep in my bed, and I can spend the night in my office."

It would be so much better if he were in bed with her. Before the shocking moment of their birth-control fail, there had been that wonderful moment of waking up in his arms. They were taking it slow, but it would be nice to experience that again. But they couldn't tonight.

She eased into a sitting position. "No. I don't think that would go over well with Carly."

Sighing, he intertwined their fingers on his thigh. "I'm sorry she was so unfriendly."

A thought crept into Bea's mind. Had Carly kept putting the container of food between them on purpose? She almost asked the question. But if Devin didn't see it that way, it would sound like she was making an accusation against his daughter. And she and Carly had already gotten off to a rocky start.

Bea mirrored back the confidence Devin had shown earlier. "Like you said, she's not going to accept us overnight. We just have to give it time."

Chapter Fifteen

Devin stood in the driveway watching Bea drive away. He'd offered to take her home, but she hadn't wanted to leave her car there.

She didn't live that far away, but he'd worry about her until he got the call or text that she'd made it safely to her condo.

Someday, hopefully soon, she'd feel comfortable enough to bring an overnight bag along when she visited and would just stay with him. But first, his daughter's attitude needed to change. If Carly would be living with him full-time, she'd have to get used to Bea and, later on, Bea and the baby being under the same roof as them.

Devin went into the house.

Carly sat curled up on the couch with a bowl of popcorn, happily watching television.

Once Bea had explained it was just the smell of the chicken in garlic sauce that had bothered her, more than a few things had fallen into place about why she'd had to leave the table at dinner.

Devin picked up the remote, turned off the television, then sat on the coffee table in front of his daughter.

"How's Bea?" Carly asked with an all-too-innocent look on her face.

"Better. So do you want to explain your behavior during dinner?"

"What do you mean?" she mumbled between bites of popcorn.

"You know *exactly* what I'm talking about. You noticed Bea had an issue with the chicken and garlic sauce, and instead of being sympathetic, you kept thrusting the container in her face. Why?"

"No, I—" Carly's expression was easy to read. Clearly she'd realized he wasn't in the mood for her shenanigans, so she wisely remained silent.

"I'm disappointed in your actions, and your mom will be, too. What you did goes against how we raised you. How would you feel if someone treated you the way you just treated Bea?"

A hint of guilt sparked behind the defiance in Carly's eyes. "You can't make me like her just because she's having a baby."

"Bea's not just having *a* baby. She's having *my* baby, who will also be your brother or sister." Devin tamped down parental frustration. Just like he was asking Carly to see things from Bea's point of view, he needed to view the situation from his daughter's.

"I love you, Carly. You're my daughter, and that will never change. But I also care about Bea and the baby, and nothing will change that, either. The only thing that can change is your attitude." He pinched the bridge of his nose, then took a slow, deep breath. "And there's something you should know. Bea was willing to assist you with your fundraising project before you treated her badly."

"She was?"

"Yes. And before she left, she still said she was willing

to help. You can think about that while you do the dishes. And after that, you can go to your room. No screen time. You have to get up early so I can take you to school in the morning."

As he rose to his feet, Devin saw tears escape from Carly's eyes. He hated seeing her upset but wouldn't coddle her. And no, he couldn't make her accept Bea or that she would have a sibling. But she knew right from wrong.

Working at the desk in his home office, he kept glancing at his phone. Shouldn't Bea have made it home by now? Was she in trouble? He stopped his mind from wandering down the road of the worst possible scenarios.

Finally, she called, and he snatched up the phone to answer it. "Hello."

"Hi. I'm home." She sounded even more tired than when she'd left. And she hadn't really eaten anything, either. Just when he was about to mention that, she added, "Sorry for not calling you as soon as I got here. I heated up a bowl of soup first."

Hearing her voice was such a relief, but the reason for her not calling him right away was a good one. "What kind?"

"Homemade chicken noodle. I made it the other night. I think I have some bread left over, too."

Good. At least she was eating something fairly substantial. "Sounds perfect." He wasn't ready to end the call yet, but she was wiped out from a long day. "Make sure you get some rest, too."

"I will."

"Good night, Bea."

"Good night."

After hanging up, Devin sat back in the chair. If he were there, he would have heated the soup for her while she took a shower or a bath. Then he would have brought it to her while she relaxed in bed. And afterward, he would have held her as she'd fallen asleep.

A longing for her tugged at his heart.

Francis whining and nudging his leg brought Devin out of his thoughts. The dog sat at his feet as if sensing his melancholy mood.

"I'm fine." Devin rubbed Francis's head and scratched behind the pup's ears.

But a small seed of self-doubt started to sprout. He'd thought he was ready for anything when it came to Bea, the baby and Carly. But could he balance being a dad of two? Was tonight's episode an indication that he couldn't?

That night, he restlessly dreamed of Bea reaching out for him. Just as he got to her, she slipped out of his arms and backed away.

When he woke up, he wished she was with him, and for more sleep. But he needed to walk Francis, and he wanted to make sure Carly had breakfast before he took her to school.

After returning from a longer-than-anticipated stroll with Francis, Devin woke up his daughter, then rushed through trimming his beard and a shower.

Oatmeal for breakfast would have been a nice healthy option. That was what Lauren would have made, but he also had to pack a bag for Francis, as he was taking the dog with him to the office. Cold cereal would have to do.

Devin set up everything on the table, then called out down the hallway, "Carly—breakfast."

She would be a while. The teen took forever to get ready in the morning.

He poured himself a mug of coffee, sat down, and

started reviewing the *Chatelaine Daily News* online edition on his phone. It had gone live earlier that morning.

Carly trudged in wearing jeans and a pink sweatshirt. She'd pulled her damp curly hair into a ponytail, fully revealing her face.

Unable to gauge her mood, he fortified himself with a sip of coffee before dealing with whatever state of mind she was in right then. "Good morning."

"Morning." She dropped into a chair at the table.

"Do you want toast?"

"No, thank you." Carly poured herself a bowl of cereal.

He switched from the online paper to his email. The first correspondence wasn't good news. A lead he'd been following on the whereabouts of Gwenyth and Renee Wells hadn't panned out. He wrote a thank-you response to the sender.

"Dad."

"Yes?"

"I'm sorry for being mean to Bea," Carly whispered.

Devin looked into her eyes. She meant it. "I appreciate the apology."

Carly toyed with the cereal floating in a bowl of milk. "I guess I should apologize to her, too."

"Yes, you should."

"I could go with you to work this morning and do it," she said.

"You're not missing school."

She offered up an exaggerated shrug. "I'm just trying to do things you and Mom raised me to do."

And she was trying to bargain like he'd done with his dad when he'd been her age. Carly was definitely his child.

Devin couldn't hold back a chuckle. "Nice try, Half Pint. Eat your cereal. We're leaving in twenty minutes."

Later that afternoon at the newspaper office, Devin multitasked at his desk, eating lunch and squeezing in a minute to work on his proposed schedule and co-parenting plan the mediator had suggested.

Carly staying with him this week was actually a bonus in helping him visualize his role as the primary parent. His days would definitely be busier, but he could handle the changes. And Carly was old enough to take on a few more responsibilities—making her own breakfast, helping to keep the house tidy and learning to do the laundry, too.

His thoughts drifted back to that morning. He was glad that Carly had said she was sorry and wanted to apologize to Bea. That type of maturity showed she was growing up.

And it was a step in the right direction. If Carly and Bea could spend time together, he just knew they'd get along. Bea was fun-loving and patient, but she could also offer a firm guiding hand if needed. She doubted her ability to become a parent, but she was more equipped than she realized.

A few minutes later, Francis paced and sniffed in front of the closed door, signaling it was time for a break.

Done with his sandwich, Devin clipped the leash onto the dog's collar, grabbed a waste bag from a stash in the desk, and headed out from the office.

Late in the afternoon, only a few pedestrians were out, and an occasional car came by as he walked Francis to an open lot with a few bushes.

The Cowgirl Café was just down the street. A couple of staff members were being dropped off for work. He'd texted Bea that morning, checking on her before he'd gone to the office. But a message wasn't the same as hearing her voice.

As he waited for Francis to mark his territory, he phoned Bea.

She answered on the third ring. "Hey, Devin."

"Hey." Holding on to the leash, he followed the pup to the next bush he was curious about. "Francis and I are taking a short walk. Can you join us?"

"I really wish I could, but I have to finish taking inventory before we open. But I can pop out for a minute and say hi. Where are you?"

"Just down the street."

"Can you meet me in the parking lot near the side door in about ten minutes?"

He reached the café with time to spare. Francis alternated between sitting and walking near him. Most likely the dog was fidgeting around because he could sense his human's mood.

Devin crouched down and petted Francis. "It's okay. I'm just excited to see my girl."

My girl... As he thought about those last two words, contentment and happiness filled him. He couldn't help but smile. And as Francis wagged his tail, he seemed to be smiling with him.

Bea came out of the restaurant carrying two white paper bags. She held them up. "This one is for Francis. And this one is yours."

"That sounds confusing. Maybe this will help clear it up." Devin swooped in for a kiss.

As they started to ease apart, Bea's lips curved into a

smile under his. "I hope it does. Otherwise you'll be eating leftover steak, and Francis will be enjoying your tartlets."

"I like tartlets, but I like the third option even more." He wrapped an arm around her waist and went back in for a longer kiss.

Francis threatening to lasso them with the leash brought it to an end.

Devin disentangled them.

"I should go back to work." Bea held out the bags.

He accepted them. "Before I forget, Carly wants to apologize to you for her behavior last night."

"Does she want to apologize, or did you tell her to?"

"She wants to." Bea's skeptical expression prompted him to say more. "The only thing I mentioned to her last night was how disappointed I was in her behavior. She knows better. This morning at breakfast, she apologized to me and said she wanted to talk to you."

"Okay—if that's what she wants. I'll be free around eight tonight if she wants to call me."

He smiled at her. "I'll let her know."

As he took a step forward, the side door opened. A couple of the café's staff members came out for a break.

Reading Bea's body language, he took a step back. It wasn't about them hiding that they were together—she was the boss and wanted to keep certain boundaries in place. He could respect that.

"Thanks for the treats. Especially that third one."

She laughed. "You're more than welcome."

Later that night, standing in the kitchen, Devin ate the last of the half dozen tartlets.

He and Carly had practically inhaled them after dinner.

Her animated voice floated in from the open sliding door. She was on the deck, talking with Bea over the phone. They'd been on the call a good fifteen minutes. The apology Carly was delivering must have been a huge one.

But the fact that it was taking so long was a positive thing, right?

The sliding door closed.

Carly breezed into the kitchen. "Bea wants to talk to you." She gave him his phone, then went back out through the other archway.

From her face, he couldn't gauge if Bea wanting to talk to him was a good or bad sign. Glancing at the screen, he was caught off guard to see Bea's image. From the background, she was in her office.

He hadn't realized it was a video call. "Hello."

"Hi." She tucked a strand of hair behind her ear. "So, we need to talk about something."

"Uh-oh, what happened?"

"Nothing bad." She laughed. "I've never heard you so serious."

"Well, Carly didn't give me a heads-up about how your talk went, so I'm not sure what to expect."

"It's all good. Or at least I think it is. Carly really liked the tartlets I gave you, and she wants me to help her make some for the bake sale. I wanted to check in with you first."

Devin leaned back against the counter. "I don't mind, as long as she's not infringing on your time. Did she tell you the bake sale is Saturday?"

"Yes, we can make them Friday afternoon. Carly said school is out an hour early for some reason?"

Was that this Friday? *Damn.* He'd thought it was next

week. A sinkhole had opened up in a neighborhood the next town over, and he'd arranged to interview some of the residents.

"Yeah," he answered. "What time do you want to come by?"

"I was hoping Carly could come to my place. I'm not working on Friday. I'll already be at home. It would easier to do it there versus bringing everything to your house."

"That works." Devin calculated times in his mind. He could drop off Carly, go do the interviews, and be back around the time they were done. "Are you sure she doesn't need to bring anything? I'm happy to pick up the ingredients you need."

"No, that's fine." Bea met his gaze. She looked tired and pretty at the same time.

"Did you eat anything besides just tasting the entrees?"

"Yes. I had an entire chicken pot pie for dinner and a salad."

"I'm glad to hear that." He wished he could go see her, but it was getting late, and he couldn't leave Carly. "Francis really enjoyed his treat."

"I'm glad. And what about his foster guardian? Did he enjoy his?"

"Too much." Devin patted his stomach. "It's a good thing Francis is here to help me get some exercise."

"So I guess that means you won't be stopping by tomorrow for another bag of treats."

A grin broke through with his chuckle. "No, I will absolutely stop by, especially if more kisses are involved."

"I think that can be arranged." Bea's soft smile intensified his anticipation.

It grew so strong, in fact, that when he met Bea the next

afternoon, he couldn't wait. As soon as she reached him, he took her in his arms.

When she met him halfway for the promised kiss, his heart leaped.

They eased back, and a soft smile even more beautiful than the one on her face last night lit up her eyes.

Taking it slow was impossible—he was already falling for her.

Chapter Sixteen

Bea double-checked the bowls, utensils, and ingredients. The binder with her mom's recipes was also on the kitchen counter.

It was almost three o'clock. Carly would be arriving soon.

As the minutes ticked by, a sense of restless anxiety hit, and Bea resisted making sure everything was in place one more time. She and Carly were just making tartlets together. Why was she so darn nervous? Like *first day of school, wondering if she could make friends* nervous. But that was a weird take on the situation. Carly was thirteen, and she was a grown woman.

Still, she couldn't deny that she wanted Carly to see her as...what? She wasn't on the verge of becoming Carly's stepmom. She was just Devin's new girlfriend. And she would be the mother of Carly's half brother or sister. Whether or not she and the teen had a connection beyond that was yet to be seen.

Bea paced away from the counter. It would be so helpful to talk to Esme right now. But the newlyweds were on a warm, tropical beach enjoying time as a family. She wasn't going to interrupt them with her fears or her problems.

The doorbell rang, and she went to the door.

Devin and Carly stood outside. The teen had a backpack slung over her shoulder and held a bouquet of flowers in her hands.

"Come in." Bea waved them inside.

"These are for you." Carly offered her the bouquet of hydrangeas, roses, and lilies. "They're from Dad.

"No, they're from *both* of us," he interjected. "As a thank-you for your time."

"They're gorgeous and much appreciated." As she lifted the fragrant bouquet to her nose, her gaze landed on his mouth, and memories of kissing him yesterday afternoon flashed through her mind.

"Can I use your bathroom?" Carly asked.

Bea gave herself a mental shake and pointed. "Sure. It's down the hall, first door on the right."

The teenager dropped her backpack onto the floor, and as she hurried off, Bea turned toward the kitchen. "I better put these in a vase."

Before she'd taken a step, Devin looped an arm around her waist and brought her back toward him.

Just like yesterday, she met him for a kiss. This time, they didn't hold back. The slow drift and glide as he explored her mouth raised a moan out of her.

Bea laid a hand on his chest and nudged him back a little. "Carly…

"She took her phone with her," he murmured against her lips. "She'll be in there at least another couple of minutes. I have something important to ask you."

"What?" she asked breathlessly.

"Lauren's coming back early from her trip. She's picking up Carly later tonight. You could pack a bag and spend the night with me."

Sweet temptation curled inside of her. She wanted to… but what about them taking it slow? "I'll think about it."

"That's fair."

But the kiss he followed up with wasn't. It conveyed what would happen if she threw caution to the wind.

Caught in the spin of ever-deepening desire, she grasped a hold of the front of his shirt.

They really had to stop. Otherwise she wouldn't be able to concentrate on baking—all she would think about was him. Reluctantly, she slipped out of his arms.

Carly opened the bathroom door and came down the hallway. As she picked up her backpack, she gave them a curious look that paused on Bea. "What happened to the flowers?"

Bea glanced at the semi-squashed bouquet and the petals on the floor. "Oh…"

"She dropped them." Devin cleared his throat. "I should get going. I don't want to miss the press conference."

"Press conference?" Bea asked.

"Another sink hole opened up a few miles north of Chatelaine. The folks in that area are up in arms, and the county officials are making a statement. I won't be gone long. Just a couple of hours or so."

Carly snorted in disbelief.

"Hey." Devin playfully shot his daughter an admonishing look. "Behave. And do what Bea tells you. And make sure you save a few tartlets for me—I have to make sure they're fit for consumption."

"Whatever, Dad." Carly gave a small eye roll as she hugged him.

Bea walked him to the door. Before he stepped out, he gave her a wink. "See you later."

"Bye." Her heart was still fluttering in her chest as she and Carly went to the kitchen.

Fortunately, most of the flowers had survived being squashed, and they brightened the nook in the kitchen.

Moments later, she and Carly were both wearing yellow aprons and had pulled back their hair.

Bea pointed to a bowl of apples. "We're making apple tartlets like we talked about, but I made some peach filling earlier today in case you wanted a variety."

"That sounds good." Carly picked up an apple. "So we're peeling them?"

"Yes, but we're making the dough for the tartlet crust first. It has to chill for at least an hour before we bake them. I hope we can get everything done before your dad gets back."

"We will. When dad's working on something for the paper, he's never on time. Mom says she always has to add an hour or more to when Dad says he's coming back. He gets distracted and forgets what he's supposed to do. We're used to it."

"Oh? That's…interesting." Was that really true?

Since she'd known Devin, he'd only been late once—the day they'd gone to pick up Francis. Maybe Carly was just parroting something Lauren had said a time or two.

Bea showed Carly how to make the dough for the crust. She was a natural at it.

Next they peeled the apples. Once Bea had demonstrated how to safely use the knife, she allowed the teen to help cut the fruit.

The chop of the knives against their cutting boards filled the silence.

Carly dropped diced apples into the bowl sitting between them on the counter. "Can I ask you a question?"

"Sure."

She hesitated an instant, then blurted out, "Are you and the baby going to live with my dad?"

Bea carefully finished dicing an apple. It was best to be honest, right? "Your father and I haven't decided on that."

Carly toyed with the peeled apple on her board but didn't cut it. "There's only two bedrooms—mine and dad's." A hint of color flushed in the girl's light brown cheeks. "His office was a bedroom…"

Bea put down her knife and turned her full attention to Carly. "No matter what we decide, you'll always have your room. No one's going to take that from you."

Carly gave her a quick smile and shrug. "I was just wondering."

Bea wanted to reach out and reassure the teen with a hug or pat on the shoulder, but they weren't at that stage yet.

What Carly had just asked was on the parenting questionnaire. Devin said they had time, but there were so many unanswered questions…including if his daughter was going to be living with him full-time. Should they wait on making any plans until after he and Lauren worked things out? Or should she and the baby be part of the conversation now?

A little over a couple of hours later, the finished tartlets were lined up on the counter.

They tasted them, and Carly's face lit up. "These are *sooo* good. Everyone's going to want one." Her smile faded a little. "Oh no—I messed up. I should have made a video or taken pictures of me making them."

"We still can. We have extra dough and filling. We just have to stage it a little."

They set up the prep area on the counter. While Carly made tartlet shells, Bea shot video clips and took candid photos. Like her dad, Carly had a good sense of humor, and it shined through.

In the midst of taking close-ups, strands of Carly's dark brown hair fell over one of her eyes. Flour was covering her hands, so she tried to blow her hair out of her face. She laughed. "It won't move."

"I've got it." On an impulse, Bea smoothed the strands behind Carly's ear.

Memories of her mom flashed in her mind, along with what she'd felt back then when she and her mother had cooked and baked together. A strong sense of caring hit Bea, and she knew what she wanted to be for Carly.

A guide. A teacher. An encourager. A protector if need be. And when she was older, a friend. She wanted Carly to know that with her, she'd always have a place to just be herself.

"Thanks." Carly smiled.

"You're welcome."

After the photos and videos were done, they cleaned up again.

Devin was still a no-show.

While Carly was in the bathroom, Bea sent him a text, asking if he was on his way.

He didn't reply.

The teen came back into the kitchen. She glanced at the phone in Bea's hand. "Did you hear from Dad?"

"No, not yet. But if you need to work on your homework… Oh, wait—it's Friday. Are you hungry? We could make dinner?"

"That's okay. Mom and I are picking up something on the way home."

"Your mom? Isn't she still on her way back from Corpus Christi?"

"Nope. She's here. I texted her your address, and she's on her way to pick me up."

Bea wasn't sure what to say. She wasn't going to stop Carly from going with her mom. "Well, we should pack up the tartlets."

They were almost finished boxing up the desserts when the doorbell rang.

"I'll get it," Bea said. Maybe that was Devin.

She opened the door.

Devin's ex-wife stood outside. With her hair pulled back in a ponytail, she was a pretty, adult version of her daughter.

She offered a hesitant smile. "Hello. I'm Lauren, Carly's mom."

Neither one of them had probably anticipated meeting this way, but it was happening.

Bea rolled with it. "Hi, I'm Bea. Come on in. Carly's still packing up the tartlets in the kitchen, but she won't be long."

Lauren walked inside. "Thanks for helping her with the bake sale." Genuine friendliness was in her tone. "I'm so tired from my trip, the best I could have done for her tonight was put sprinkles and chocolate chips on some store-bought cupcakes. I hope it wasn't too much trouble."

"Not at all. I enjoyed it. And Carly did most of the work. Come see what she did."

They went to the kitchen.

Carly showed her mom the tartlets.

"Wow!" Lauren exclaimed. "Those look amazing. Great job. They're going to sell out before the first hour of the bake sale."

"I know." Carly beamed.

"We'll have to be careful taking them home." Lauren handed the teen her car keys. "The thermal bag I use for groceries is padded. It's behind the back seat. Go ahead and put your backpack in the car now."

Carly left the kitchen.

The front door shut, and Bea and Lauren stood silently in the kitchen.

The dark-haired woman offered up a small smile. "I really do appreciate you helping Carly. I hope Devin didn't dump the task on you and leave."

"No, it was fine. He didn't need to be here."

"But he should have gotten back in time to pick her up. As soon as Carly told me he was working on a story, I knew what happened." Hints of exasperation filled Lauren's face. "When he's caught up in a story, everyone around him gets shut out. Nothing else matters."

Nothing else? On a reflex Bea almost laid a hand on her stomach, but she caught herself.

But not before Lauren noticed. Her exasperation morphed into a swift explanation. "I'm not saying Devin's a bad guy. He's just—"

The front door opened, and Lauren grew silent.

Carly returned, and Bea shifted her attention to helping her pack the bag.

As the three of them stood at the door, the girl looked from Bea to her mom as if unsure what to do next.

Lauren motioned to Carly. "What are you waiting for? Give Bea a hug and say thank you."

"Thank you."

"You're welcome." Bea followed Carly's lead into an embrace. Happiness filled her as the teen tightened her arms around her.

After Lauren and Carly left, she leaned back against the door. Happiness faded. Where was Devin? Was he okay?

He gets distracted and forgets what he's supposed to do. We're used to it...

When he's caught up in a story, everyone around him gets shut out. Nothing else matters...

Carly and Lauren's comments played through her mind.

I'm not saying Devin's a bad guy. He's just—

He's just what? As Bea pondered the question, remnants of the doubt she'd felt years ago when she'd first noticed cracks in her marriage started to surface. *No.* This wasn't the same situation. She just needed to voice her concerns to Devin. He'd understand.

A rapping on the door startled her out of her thoughts, and she opened the door.

Devin's expression was filled with genuine remorse. "Bea, I'm sorry." He glanced down as he rubbed the back of his head. "Will you let me explain what happened?"

The first step in being able to voice her concerns was listening. Bea opened the door wider and let him in. After shutting it, she faced him, but she left her hand on the doorknob.

Devin held up his hands in surrender. "I realize none of what I'm about to say is a good excuse. I should have made it back when I said I would. But the press conference started late. And then I had people to interview. One of them gave me a lead on another story, and I made a stop to follow up on it. That side trip took longer than I anticipated."

"Why didn't you respond to my text and tell me that?"

"My phone was on silent." He grimaced. "It's a habit. When I was starting out as a cub reporter, my phone rang in the middle of an important interview. I lost the exclusive, and I almost lost my job. Ever since then, I've made sure that didn't happen again. Usually, I remember to change the setting back to normal, but I didn't until a little while ago. That's when I saw I missed your text as well as Lauren's."

He looked so sincere, but…

Devin took a step toward her. "Rather than texting or calling you back, I wanted to explain face-to-face."

Telling him what Lauren and Carly had claimed about him would sound like an accusation. And she wasn't trying to start a fight. This also wasn't about his ex-wife or his daughter—this moment was about them and their relationship.

Bea released the doorknob and walked closer to Devin. "I understand your work is important, but what if something had happened to Carly or me and we really needed to reach you? You can't go MIA like that. I was worried." Admitting that aloud made her heart constrict in her chest.

"In the future, I won't chase the next story." Devin took hold of her hand. "And I'll answer my phone. I promise."

Bea gave in to the need to be closer to him, and he immediately took her into his arms.

Kissing her temple, Devin's chest rose and fell with a deep breath. As she laid her head to his chest, their breathing synced.

He held her a bit tighter. “Thanks again for helping Carly. Lauren said she’s really excited about showing off what the two of you made tomorrow.”

“I’m glad,” she murmured.

“I am bummed that I missed out on being the official taste tester.”

The desire to be with him was undeniable, and Bea weighed whether to give in to it. “I still have ingredients left.” She leaned away and looked up at him. “We can make them at your place.”

Chapter Seventeen

A light breeze blowing heat and a bit of smoke from the grill on the back deck at Devin's house brought him out of a happy trance. If he didn't keep his mind on what he was doing, the steaks he was cooking for him and Bea would burn.

But he couldn't stop looking at her through the window into the kitchen, where she was making salad to go with dinner.

He'd thought Bea wouldn't want to come back to his place after he'd shown up late. But thankfully, she'd forgiven him, despite how badly he'd screwed up. In the future, he would be more present. He had to find a better way to balance his duties to the newspaper and being there for everyone. Or he could lose Bea, and the chance to have more wonderful moments like tonight in the future.

The experience of preparing a meal together was even better than he'd imagined. From the moment they'd walked into his house, their actions had been synced. She'd instinctively known where everything was, or he'd anticipated what she'd needed before she'd asked. It was as if Bea had always been there...that she belonged in this house with him.

He finished grilling the steaks and went inside.

As Bea put the salad into bowls, Francis watched intently as if he was enamored with her. Devin chuckled to himself. He couldn't blame him.

Bea glanced over her shoulder. "Perfect timing. I made buttered toast. I tried to make garlic toast, but..." She laughed. "It's so weird to not be able to stand garlic anymore. Roasted garlic on the grill would have been great with the steaks. I feel like I'm depriving you of the good stuff."

Devin walked up behind her and kissed Bea on the cheek. "You're not depriving me of anything, sweetheart."

Bea leaned slightly into him. She was the perfect fit, and it took everything within him not to slide his arm around her waist and mold her backside to his front. He had the good stuff. Her—within arm's reach instead of miles away.

Devin set the platter with steaks on the stove, then opened the oven to grab the baking sheet with the golden-brown triangles of toast. "Everything's ready. Let's eat."

After dinner, while Bea made the tartlets for dessert, Devin took Francis on his last walk for the night. The anticipation of returning to Bea intertwined with a sense of contentment that she would be there, waiting for him.

Needing to express what he felt, he spoke to the dog, who was wagging his tail as they walked home. "Francis, I'm a lucky man."

And he hoped to stay that way by avoiding the missteps he made earlier. The last thing he wanted to do was hurt the people he cared about, including Bea. Today was a sign. He had to do better.

Back at the house, Devin came in through the garage.

After washing up at the sink in the laundry room, he joined Bea in the kitchen.

The promised tartlets were on a platter, and she was topping them with whipped cream.

He joined her at the counter.

The sweet scent of vanilla wafted in the air.

"Ready for dessert?" she asked.

This time, as he slid his hand around her waist from behind, Devin gave in to the need of feeling her flush against him. "Uh-huh."

Looking over her shoulder, she fed him a peach tartlet, and the flaky, fruit-filled pastry filled his mouth.

"That's good..." he murmured.

"Was it worth waiting for?"

"Absolutely." Devin loosened his hold as she turned to face him.

Her gaze met his as she cupped his cheek. "Let me see." Bea briefly pressed her mouth to his, gently sucking on his lower lip as she eased away. "Oh, yeah—that's perfect."

She pressed his mouth back to his. Her teasing and slow, sweetly torturous kisses unleashed a hunger inside of him.

Devin cupped his hands to her butt, kneading her soft curves. Bea followed his lead as he lifted her up, and she wrapped her legs around him.

He wasn't just lucky. He was the luckiest man on Earth.

As Devin carried Bea down the hall, she abandoned worry and doubt. No, they didn't have forever to make important decisions, but tonight they could wait. They could embrace time.

In his bedroom, removing each other's clothes became

a slow exploration. Feather-light caresses and needy kisses followed each piece of clothing that fell to the floor.

When they were finally skin to skin on the bed, Bea longed so desperately to feel him inside of her, but he made her wait, exploring every inch, every sensitive spot on her body until she burned with erotic sensation.

Devin murmured near her ear. "You're beautiful."

And she truly felt beautiful and wholly desired by Devin as he worshipped her with more kisses and caresses that intensified her need for him.

Bea writhed and bowed up. "Devin…please…"

Holding her gaze, he slowly entered her. He moved his hips, igniting pleasure in places she'd never known existed. As she reached her orgasm, Bea felt as if every barrier, every wall of protection had splintered apart. All that was left was him. Wanting him. Needing him. Falling for him. Even possibly on the verge of loving him.

Afterward, wrapped in his arms, unease crept into her contentment. She'd trusted and believed in her ex-husband. And she'd overlooked his faults so many times, only for him to let her down? What if Devin was the same way, but she was blinded by how much she cared for him? What if she was wrong about him, too?

Pushing the thought aside, she snuggled up against him, searching for peace in the warmth of his embrace and the steady beat of his heart.

Soon, Bea fell asleep. She dreamed of holding a baby that resembled Devin in a room filled with friends and family. But he wasn't there. Suddenly the room was empty, and it was just her and the crying child.

Awakening in a sweat, she disentangled herself from Devin's arms and sat up.

Half asleep, he rasped, "You okay?"

"Yes, I'm fine." She slipped out of bed, threw on his T-shirt, and went into the bathroom.

After cooling her face down with water from the sink, she stared at her reflection in the mirror. "It was just a bad dream. I'm not alone," she whispered. "That won't happen."

But what if it did?

The next morning, fatigue and last night's dream hovered over Bea as she made her way to the kitchen.

Devin glanced over at her from where he stood at the counter. While she was still wearing his shirt that she'd slept in, he was dressed in a gray T-shirt and black athletic shorts, looking sexy as ever.

"You're up. I was just about to bring you a cup of coffee and some tea." He held up two mugs. "I wasn't sure which one you wanted, so I made both."

Walking over to him, Bea swiped the remains of the dream from her thoughts. Worry was on overdrive in her mind for no reason. "Coffee, please."

He handed her one of the mugs, and she kissed him. "Thank you."

"You're welcome. Hey—when I came back from walking Francis, I heard your phone buzzing in your purse. It sounded like more than one text message coming in."

"Really?" She paused to take a sip of coffee. "Maybe it's Tanya."

"What time are you supposed to be at the café?"

"Around one."

"That soon..." Leaning back against the counter, Devin took hold of her waist and brought her closer. "We need to plan for an entire weekend together. Maybe an overnight trip. We could drive to Corpus Christi or even fly out to Dallas."

Uninterrupted time with Devin would be heavenly. "Either one sounds nice to me."

Her phone rang in the living room.

Sighing, Bea reluctantly stepped out of his arms. "I better answer that."

In the living room, she dug her phone from her purse. It was her brother. He never called…unless it was important.

She answered. "Hi, Asa."

"Hey—sorry to interrupt your morning, but did you hear the news?"

From his tone, it wasn't good. Her heart dropped. "Did something happen to Esme or Ryder? Or the boys?"

"No—as far as I know, they're fine. It's Wendell. He fell at the house late last night and was rushed to the county hospital. A group text went out about it."

"I haven't checked my messages yet." Worry trickled through her. "How is he?"

"Lily and I went to see him this morning. From what I've heard, he's going to be fine, but all the bumps and bruises he sustained are taking a toll on him. A simple fall can become a serious thing at his age. Everyone in the family has been asked to check on him."

"Okay, I will. Thanks for letting me know."

They said their goodbyes.

Bea looked through her text messages and found the one Asa had mentioned. She glanced at Devin standing in the archway to the kitchen.

"Everything okay?" he asked.

"No. It's Wendell."

Devin joined her by the couch. "What happened?"

"He fell last night and had to be rushed to the emergency room. He was admitted to the hospital. Asa and Lily went to see him this morning."

"I'm sorry to hear that." A concerned look came over Devin's face as he sat on the arm of the couch. "I really hope..."

"What?"

"The day we went to pick up Francis from the shelter, when we were in the car, I mentioned to you that I had visited Wendell at Fortune's Castle."

She frowned. "You did? I don't remember that."

"You had a lot on your mind. I made a joke about aliens from Venus just to get your attention. Anyway, when I went to see him, I asked him about Clint Wells, the foreman who'd worked at the silver mine during the accident. The conversation seemed to upset him."

"What did he say?"

Devin shook his head. "Nothing really. I've been trying to find someone who knows the whereabouts of Clint's wife and daughter. Wendell said he didn't."

The identity of the fifty-first miner. Edgar and Elias's part in the collapse of the mine. Now the foreman's family. Too many unanswered questions still remained about the silver mine collapse. But she also got the sense that Wendell knew more than he let on.

Bea stepped between Devin's legs and laid a hand on his shoulder. "I honestly don't think your conversation with Wendell put him in the hospital. He's been sick off and on for a while."

"Well, I hope he pulls through."

"I do, too. Everyone in the family has been urged to go

and see him." She took a step back. "I'd like to drop by and visit him before I go to work. The hospital is across town from here. I should probably leave now."

"You should. That way you won't have to rush to get to the café on time." Devin stood. "I'll make you something to go for breakfast. What are you in the mood for? A smoothie? Some oatmeal?"

"A smoothie would be nice, but you don't have to make me anything."

"Yes, I do." He kissed her forehead and rested his hand on her stomach.

A sense of feeling wholly protected by Devin came over her. It would be so easy to get used to him taking care of her, but maybe she shouldn't. Yes, they were getting along, but there was still so much for them to figure out.

Still, she lingered until he let her go.

On the way to the bedroom, Bea paused. "The Wells family—have you found anything about them?"

"Just a bunch of dead ends." Resignation was in Devin's raised brow expression. "They don't want to be found. And maybe that's the way it should be."

Chapter Eighteen

Bea stood by Wendell's bedside in a private room at County General Hospital. As he slept, his breathing was steady, but he looked so frail, and his face had an unhealthy pallor.

She gently took his hand. "Hi, Wendell. It's Bea. I'm just going to sit here and visit with you for a bit."

The dark-haired nurse checking his IV glanced over at her. "He's doing well. He's on pain medication, so don't be alarmed if he doesn't wake up while you're here or if he wakes up in a daze."

"Thank you for letting me know."

"You're welcome." The nurse left.

Empathy filled Bea as she looked at Wendell. The poor man. It was too bad that he didn't have children of his own to look after his welfare. That made it even more crucial for her and the rest of the family to be there for him.

As she moved to sit down in the chair by the bed, Wendell's hand grasped her fingers.

"I'm sorry..." His eyes remained closed as he mumbled, "I should have done right by you. I should have done better."

"You have done right be me." She patted his arm. "It's okay."

"No..." As he shook his head, his breathing grew a little heavier. "I didn't. I should have acknowledged you publicly as my own instead of hiding from it."

The nurse's warning about him possibly waking up in a daze was accurate. He was clearly mixing her up with someone else.

Bea lightly squeezed his hand. "Wendell, I'm Bea, your niece. Bea Fortune."

Wendell's eyes opened, and he stared up at her with a confused look that became shadowed by a pained expression. "Don't hate me. I was just trying to do what I thought was best. I know you loved him, but he was destitute...a miner. I just wanted a better life for you...you're my child..."

His *what*? Was Wendell saying he had a daughter? Maybe an illegitimate one, from the sounds of it.

"Wendell..." She gave his hand another light squeeze. "Who are you talking about? What's her name?"

His eyes fluttered closed with a sigh, and as his hand went slack in hers, his breathing grew steady.

That was weird. Had she heard him right? No one had ever mentioned to her about Wendell having a daughter. Had he kept this secret from everyone...until now?

Moments later, sitting in the car, she struggled to make sense of what he'd said. In his dazed state of mind, maybe he had told this to someone else. Glancing through the names and numbers associated with the test message alerting the family he'd been hurt, she debated who to call.

Aunt Freya maybe? But what if she didn't know about him possibly having a child? This could potentially be a bombshell for her and maybe everyone else on the list.

One name caught her eye. Tabitha Buckingham. She was family via the twins, but she was also the most neutral party connected to the Fortunes. Talking to her might help. And Bea had been meaning to reach out to her anyway. She could squeeze in at least a half hour or so visit before she went to the café.

Bea gave Tabitha a call.

"Sure, come on over. I could use some adult company," Tabitha said. "But fair warning—I'm in the middle of folding laundry, so it's a little messy."

Bea arrived at Tabitha's house. Just as the young mother had claimed, stacks of folded laundry along with baskets of unfolded clothes took up most of the living room couch.

Tabitha's blond hair was tied back. Dressed in yoga pants and a T-shirt, she was in casual mom mode, and from the flush in her cheeks, she'd been busy.

Bea glanced around. "Where are the twins?"

"Napping."

"Oh..." She lowered her voice.

Tabitha waved her off. "You're good. When they're conked out, unless there's shouting, nothing wakes them up." She moved a basket of unfolded laundry and set it on the coffee table, before perching on the end of the couch. "Please have a seat."

Bea settled into the spot she'd cleared for her. "Would you like a hand?"

"I would love one."

As they started sorting and stacking bibs, blankets, socks, sleepers and onesies, Bea was reminded of the newborn-essentials checklist.

She'd emailed the checklist to Devin along with the parenting questionnaire, but he hadn't said anything about them. Maybe she should have reminded him? But shouldn't he have remembered their conversation and mentioned them to her or at least acknowledged he'd received them? He'd mentioned last night that he'd finished the parenting plan for Carly. Wasn't the parenting questionnaire for their baby just as important? Or was she being selfish…?

"This is a nice surprise." Tabitha added a folded bib to the stack on the coffee table. "But from the look on your face, you have something on your mind."

Bea debated how to dive into the topic. "You saw the text about Wendell?"

"I did. But I have to admit, I've been so busy with the twins, I haven't even gotten a chance to really read it. Something about a fall?"

"Yes, he's in the hospital, but he's recovering."

"I'm so glad to her that. At his age, falls can be a scary thing. I wish I had time to go visit him now, but I'm behind on so many things, including the laundry, and I'm playing catch up. And then both Zach and Zane ended up with the diaper rash from hell. This week I wasn't sure if I was coming or going. And then…" Chuckling, she shook her head. "Sorry, I didn't mean to unload on you like that. You were saying…?"

Although she'd come here intending to discuss Wendell's dazed confession, after seeing Tabitha now, she had a change of heart. The young mom had said she'd needed some adult conversation, not speculation and gossip about things that weren't even on her radar.

Bea added a folded onesie to the stack beside her on the couch. "It's not important. So is the diaper rash from hell gone?"

"Yes, thank goodness! I had to remind my babysitter about sticking to the diapering routine. I need and appreciate her help, but it only makes it harder for me if she's not on board with my routines. It's tough."

"Other than managing the babysitter, how are you? And be honest. It's okay to gripe… I don't mind."

Tabitha's shoulders fell as she released a slow breath. "Honestly, what I wish I had and need the most is West." Her gaze strayed to the framed photo next to a baby monitor on the side table.

In the picture, the golden-haired couple were a striking pair. And they looked so happy.

Tabitha added. "But even if he was here, we wouldn't be together." Hints of sadness filled her tone.

"What? No—what makes you say that?"

"One, West never wanted children. And two, we broke up the night before he died. I had no idea I was pregnant at the time."

"But don't you think he would have wanted to know his children? That he might have changed his mind once the twins arrived?"

Tabitha gave her a slightly tremulous smile. "I don't know if his mind would have changed. He might have adapted to the situation, but West's job dominated his time." She sighed. "And honestly, I'm not sure I could have handled me and the twins coming in second or third to a never-ending list of trials or another tough case. And I loved him too much to make him choose. He might have done it, but he also might have resented me for it later on. I wouldn't have wanted to take that risk."

"So you might have chosen to be a single mom? It can't be easy."

Tabitha offered up a small shrug. "It's difficult to say. But I do know losing West the way I did was the hardest thing of all. I'm so lucky to have the twins. At least I have a part of him."

Bea's heart went out to the other woman, but she also admired her strength. "Yes, you do. And you're doing a great job raising them."

Tabitha smiled. "Thanks—I needed to hear that today. Sure, being a single mom is hard sometimes. But like I said, I've developed routines. I eat when they eat. I sleep when they sleep, or I catch up on laundry and housework. I make it work. And I have a network of friends that I can call on. But trust me, this isn't the most nerve-racking part of having kids." Humor filled her eyes. "Some people might think I've lost my mind by saying this, but I'll gladly take all of the chaos I have now over being pregnant. Now, that was scary. Unless you've been through it, nothing can prepare you."

"I know—I'm pregnant."

A shocked smile came over Tabitha's face. "You are? Oh my gosh! When did you find out?"

"Just recently," Bea admitted. "But you're the first family member I've told."

"Don't worry. I won't breathe a word to anyone. So are you happy, or are you…"

"Well… I'm definitely scared and…" A feeling Bea had never felt since finding out she was pregnant surfaced. "Thrilled?"

Tabitha laughed. "That's so normal." She quickly set the laundry aside. Moving closer, she took Bea's hand. "Tell me everything…"

Bea poured out her excitement and fears. Tabitha listened, answered her questions, and gave her advice on everything from how to handle morning sickness to pregnancy books to maternity clothes.

A cry from one of the twins came through the baby monitor. Then the second joined in.

"It's time to feed my boys." Tabitha tilted her head toward the hallway. "Do you want to see them?"

Bea hesitated. She really needed to head to the café soon. "I do."

In the nursery, Bea smiled and cooed at the light-haired twins along with Tabitha. She helped changed their diapers, and when Tabitha handed her a bottle, Bea settled into one of the rocking chairs with Zach in her arms.

Looking into his eyes, Bea saw her world in the future. *I'll have support. I won't be alone.* But as scared as she was, she couldn't wait to meet her baby.

Later that night in her bedroom, on a video call with Devin, Bea told him about her visit to see Wendell at the hospital.

She propped up the pillows behind her back on the headboard. "I'm really baffled by what Wendell told me. If he has an illegitimate daughter someplace, where is she?"

Devin was outside walking Francis. "That is strange."

"I don't know. Maybe I should ask someone if they know anything."

"Hold on a sec." Devin turned his attention from the phone. "Francis…" he said in a warning tone. "Sorry—someone else is walking their dog. What did you say?"

"I was wondering if maybe I should ask someone if they know anything."

"And if no one does, you're back at square one, trying

to get answers from Wendell. And with his health the way it is, do you really want to broach that topic with him?"

"That's true." Her thoughts drifted to Tabitha. "I went to see my twin nephews today—Zach and Zane. They're a little over ten months old and so adorable."

"Really?" From the background change, Devin was entering his house. "Twins. That's a lot."

"Their mom, Tabitha, has a good routine. She says routines are important."

"Yeah, that helps." He propped up the phone on the counter as he took care of Francis.

"She gave me lots of ideas. And I love her nursery setup. She has a small refrigerator and counter space for a bottle warmer and feeding supplies. And on the other side of the room is the changing station. Seeing her setup inspired me, so I looked online and found a room design that I think will go well here. I'm sending you the page link."

"Sounds…nice." He picked up his phone again, but from the distance in his voice, something else was on his mind.

"And she hired a really good babysitter from Venus."

He gave her a lopsided smile. "I was paying attention. You like her nursery."

"You were *half* paying attention. Is something bothering you, or am I bothering you?"

"No, you're not bothering me." As he briefly looked away, he paused. "It's Lauren. She's postponing our next meeting with the mediator. We were supposed to present our co-parenting plans. We can't drag our feet on making this decision. And it feels like that's what she's doing." He blew out an agitated breath. "And I even told her that over the next two weeks, my schedule was going to be busier with Quinn taking days off one week and Charles the next."

Bea's excitement about her visit with Tabitha faded. She'd hoped maybe Devin would pull up the link on his laptop now so they could share ideas. "I'm sorry to hear that."

He shook his head. "As always with Lauren, it's complicated. I'm sorry for being so distracted. Next time we talk, I'll be in a better headspace. I promise."

They said good night, and as Bea pulled up the covers, unease settled in with her again.

Devin kept making promises to her. But what was that saying? The more promises you made—the more chances you took to break them.

Chapter Nineteen

Tanya pointed to three plates of scrambled eggs on the table in the dining room of the café. She was perfecting the breakfast and brunch catering menus and wanted Bea's opinion. "The first plate is just eggs, butter, salt, and pepper. The second batch has cream added to it. The third has eggs, milk, butter, salt and pepper, and cheddar cheese."

"They all look good." Bea picked up her fork.

She tasted the food samples, but her thoughts felt as scrambled as the eggs on the plates. As much as she wanted to focus on this Wednesday-morning taste test, that past weekend and the last couple of days with Devin kept playing through her mind.

Since Saturday, he'd been distant and preoccupied. And his afternoon walks this week with Francis hadn't included a stop by the café. Although he had said he was coming by that afternoon. But when they did talk, the conversation always veered away from them toward the newspaper or issues with Lauren.

"So what do you think?" Tanya asked.

Bea brought her thoughts back to the task at hand, and she sampled the last plate. "I like plate number one and number three."

"Perfect." Tanya smiled as she got up. "Those two are the most popular with everyone who's tasted them, and they were my choice, too. The catering menu should be finalized in a few days. And the Belgian waffle makers I ordered are on the way. You know, chicken and waffles might be something to add to the dinner menu in the future."

"I like that possibility. We'll revisit that when the time comes." Bea added it to the notes on her digital tablet. Chicken and waffles wasn't an entrée her mom had made, but being open to new things would keep the menu fresh and interesting.

Bea returned to her office.

She and Tanya had also finished the new shelf diagrams for how the food should be organized in the walk-ins. They needed to be printed out. But her printer was out of paper, and the stash in her desk was gone, too.

Bea searched the storage room down the hall where they kept office supplies. But she didn't see a box of printer paper or reams stacked on the shelf. They couldn't have used all of the paper that fast. As she stepped back for a wider view, she spotted the packages on the top shelf out of reach.

Really? Bea let out a long breath. Putting the paper on a lower shelf made more sense, especially since they used it on a regular basis.

As she made a mental note to mention this to the stock person, Bea grabbed the small stepladder in the corner. After setting it up near the shelf, she climbed up, but she couldn't quite reach the copy paper.

A taller stepladder was in the dining room storage closet, but she just needed one package.

Raising up onto her toes, she reached up, and her fingertips grazed the side of one of the packs, knocking it askew. *Almost got it...* She stretched her arm higher and slid it out a bit further.

But instead of just one, a domino of reams broke free.

"No!" A package started falling toward her head, and when she ducked out of the way, her foot slipped off the stepladder.

As she landed hard on the floor, horror consumed her mind. *The baby...!*

Devin sat with Quinn in his office. He'd asked her to do some research on the Wells family, but the results were less than promising.

"It's like they disappeared." Quinn shrugged. "I searched birth and death announcements, real estate purchases, old addresses. Nothing is coming up for Clint Wells's family in the surrounding area. Do you want me to widen the search?"

Did he want to keep digging for answers? Devin was tempted, but the rabbit hole of searching for answers about the miners seemed endless. And the one person who probably knew the truth—Wendell Fortune—wasn't talking.

Devin shook his head. "We're going to have to press the pause button on this story for now."

She stood. "I don't blame the West family for disappearing after all they went through. If I were them, I would have gotten as far as possible from Texas and never looked back."

As Quinn left, Devin studied the document on his desktop screen listing the leads he and his assistant had checked into. All of them were dead ends. *And maybe that's the way it should be...*

That was what he'd told Bea. Quinn not finding anything could be a sign to follow that advice.

Devin closed the file on the Fortunes' silver mine, then opened the one he'd created with the co-parenting plan documents. He hadn't downloaded the newborn-essentials checklist and the parenting questionnaire Bea had sent him, but he still had plenty of time to get them done.

The checklist would be easy. He'd make sure Bea had whatever she wanted for the baby. And the questionnaire probably resembled the one he and Lauren had filled out regarding Carly during their divorce mediation.

It had questions like, who would be your primary-care physician? Carly's pediatric physician was great. That would be his recommendation. Healthcare and medical expenses? Again, that was easy. He could take care of it all, or if Bea wanted to split the responsibilities, he wouldn't object. Which parent would be the child's "home base?" That was the most important question on that list.

A vision of him, Bea, the baby, and Carly living together as a family came into his mind. The possibility of that made him smile.

Carly and Bea had gotten along well making the tartlets for the bake sale. Maybe, despite his lingering doubts, his vision of a family wasn't as far off as it seemed.

A text from his ex-wife dinged on his phone.

Can we meet at my house in an hour?

Devin glanced at the clock on the screen. He'd left Francis at home today, but he'd told Bea he would stop by later that afternoon. Whatever it was, he could probably meet Lauren and make it back in time.

A follow-up text appeared on the screen.

It's important.

When *wasn't* it important with Lauren?

Meet you there.

Unease and frustration accompanied him on the drive. He had no idea what Lauren had to tell him, but he sensed it wasn't going to be good.

When he arrived at the house and walked inside, Lauren's stubborn expression confirmed it.

Carly was at school, and the house was quiet.

The taps of his ex-wife's heels echoed as they walked into the kitchen and seemed magnified in the silence. Her keys, phone, and business tote were on the counter. From the looks of things, she'd come from work.

She faced him. "There's no easy way to say this, so I'll just be direct. They need me in Corpus Christi sooner. I wanted to work out a custody arrangement with you through a mediator, but I don't see the point under the circumstances."

He crossed his arms over his chest. "No, a change in your timetable doesn't change the circumstances of us coming to an agreement."

"That's not the circumstance I'm talking about. You're about to have a baby with another woman. It's a new responsibility."

"That has nothing to do with me taking care of Carly."

"It does. You can barely make time for her now. I have to fill in the gaps."

Devin's frustration broke through. "That's bullshit. You were gone practically a whole week, and we did just fine. In fact, Carly and I have done just fine anytime you've left town. You're just trying to come up with excuses for why you should take her to Corpus Christi."

"I don't need an excuse. And I think a judge will agree with me."

"A *judge*?" Disbelief made him pause.

His phone rang, and he took it from his pocket.

"See what I mean?" Lauren pointed at him. "You can't even focus on a conversation about our daughter without distractions."

Not recognizing the number on the screen, he ignored the call, put the phone on silent, and tossed it onto the counter next to hers.

Irritation and calmness brewed inside of him. "You want to see me focused. I can build just as strong of a case. You'll be a single parent with a new job in a new city. You talk about filling in the gaps? Who are you going to call in Corpus Christi when you can't pick Carly up from an afterschool event or when you have to go away on a business trip?"

Lauren advanced on him. "You—"

"Stop fighting!" Carly screamed.

Startled, he and Lauren both looked toward the living room where their daughter stood.

Her face was pale, and her eyes were wide.

Devin's stomach plummeted. What was she doing home? Had she been here the entire time?

"Sweetie." Lauren rushed from the kitchen, and he wasn't far behind. "It's not what you think—"

Carly backed away from her mom. "We're *moving*? Why didn't you tell me?"

"I was waiting for the right time," Lauren began.

"So that's it?" Tears sprang from the teen's eyes. "You get to decide everything? What about what I want?"

Devin stepped ahead of Lauren "We know this is a surprise for you, but we just—"

"You and mom don't know anything!" Carly stormed past them to the back sliding door and left the house.

Devin looked at Lauren.

As she pressed her hands to her cheeks, she looked as stricken as he felt. "I didn't see her. I didn't look. I just assumed she was at school. She *should* be at school."

An accusation almost slipped out of him. Devin released a harsh breath as he massaged his neck. He couldn't find fault with Lauren's actions. He should have paid better attention when he'd walked into the house. They both should have—instead of going at each other.

"Her skipping school is the least of our worries," he said wearily. "We should go talk to her."

Lauren stalled him with a raised hand. "I can fix this now. I'll just turn down the job."

He was tempted to agree but knew that wouldn't be fair. "Taking away her right to decide by making a choice you don't want won't fix this situation. We need to listen to what she has to say."

They went outside.

Carly sat on the edge of the pool with her feet in the water.

Devin took off his boots and socks, rolled up his jeans, and Lauren kicked off her heels and rolled up her pant legs.

He sat on one side of Carly and put his feet in the water, and Lauren did the same on the other side of her.

Carly kicked up the water, soaking their legs.

As the long seconds passed, memories of playing games in the pool with Carly when she'd been younger, and of her infectious laughter floated through his thoughts.

"I'm sorry," Lauren said softly. "We should have told you. We were just trying to work things out with a mediator first."

Carly kicked the water harder. "You said you were going to a judge."

Lauren looked to him for help.

Devin replied, "That was something that came up today, but we started working with a mediator last Monday. He wanted me and your mom to make up schedules and parenting plans for either choice—if you stayed here with me or went with your mom to Corpus Christi."

She turned to Lauren. "You think Corpus Christi is better for me even though my friends are here?"

"I just want you to experience more opportunities. A bigger school with more activities would do that. But I can understand if you don't want to leave your friends."

Carly looked to Devin. "And you think I should stay here instead of doing new things?"

"No. I want you to try new things. But I know you were looking forward to going to high school here and playing volleyball or maybe joining the cheerleading squad. I didn't want you to miss out on that."

"Would the choice have been mine?"

Devin glanced at Lauren. From the look in her eyes, they were on the same page. "It is starting now. What do you want to do? Stay here, or go to Corpus Christi?"

Carly stared down at the water, then said, "And whatever I choose, you won't be mad at me?"

As Lauren wrapped an arm around her, she blinked back tears. "Of course not. Your dad and I love you." Resignation was in her eyes as she glanced over at Devin. And in that moment, he knew she wouldn't fight him about Carly staying in Chatelaine.

He nudged Carly's shoulder with his. "Your mom's right. We love you and we only want the best for you, whatever that may be."

Carly nodded. "Okay." She looked up and met his gaze. "I want to go to Corpus Christi."

Lauren's mouth dropped open in surprise.

Disappointment and disbelief pushed a sharp exhale out of him. He quickly recovered and forced a smile. "Then Corpus Christi it is."

"But I still get to come home and see you, right?"

Home... The reassurance that one word gave choked him up for a few long seconds. "Yeah, definitely. We'll figure it out."

"Can we talk about it now?" Carly asked.

"Sure. Just let me call Quinn and let her know I'm not coming back to the office."

Devin walked inside the house. Mixed emotions sat heavy in his chest. In the kitchen, he closed his eyes and breathed.

Lauren joined him. "I don't know what to say..."

"There's nothing to say. I just want Carly to be happy. And if that's in Corpus Christi with you, I can live with that." He picked up his phone. Noticing the missed voice mail, he listened to it.

"Devin, it's Freya Fortune. There was an accident at the café…"

Chapter Twenty

"I'm fine." Bea looked at Freya standing next to the bed in the treatment bay at the emergency room. "I stumbled off the step stool and twisted my ankle. That's all."

When she'd first landed on the ground, she'd been more afraid for the baby. But after a moment or two, she'd realized everything was probably okay with the pregnancy and that she'd just hurt herself.

"But you also bumped the back of your head on the shelf." Genuine concern filled Freya's expression. "It could be more serious than you think."

One of the kitchen staff had heard the commotion in the storeroom and found Bea sprawled on the floor. She'd convinced everyone not to call an ambulance, but the older woman had insisted on driving her to the county hospital.

The curtain opened, and the emergency room physician came in carrying an electronic tablet. "Hello. I'm Doctor Hanson. You're Bea Fortune?"

"Yes."

The dark-haired woman wearing a white hospital coat turned to Freya. "And you are?"

"I'm her aunt. And I'm not going anywhere." The look on her face dared anyone to tell her otherwise.

"As long as it's okay with Ms. Fortune."

Bea nodded. “She can stay.”

Dr. Hanson consulted the tablet. “It says here that you experienced a fall in your restaurant and hurt your left ankle?”

“And she hit her head,” Freya chimed in.

“But not that hard,” Bea objected. As the doctor examined her ankle, she winced. “It’s a little tender.”

Dr. Hanson checked the back of Bea’s head. “Have you felt dizzy or disoriented since the fall?”

“No. Nothing like that. Not even a headache.”

The doctor took a pen light from the pocket of her coat. “Follow my finger.”

Bea complied, looking left to right then up and down.

“If you’re head does start to hurt or you feel dizzy, let us know.” Dr. Hansen pointed to Bea’s ankle. “Most likely you suffered a sprain. But I would like to take a couple of quick X-rays to be sure.”

Alarm ran through Bea, and she placed her hand over her abdomen. “You can’t.”

“Don’t be so stubborn.” Freya scoffed. “It’s a precaution. Why not be sure?”

“I’m not being stubborn. And I am being cautious.” This wasn’t the way Bea wanted to announce the news, but… “I’m pregnant.”

Freya’s eyes widened.

Dr. Hanson scrolled through information on her screen. “I was just about to ask you if you were. You didn’t indicate yes or no on your form.”

“In the midst of everything… I must have missed the question.” Embarrassment sent a rush of heat into Bea’s face. Did that make her a bad mom?

“How far along are you?” Dr. Hanson asked.

"Less than a month. I had a blood test to confirm it a couple of weeks ago."

An understanding expression crossed the doctor's face. "Have you set up an appointment to start prenatal care?"

"Yes."

"Good." She gave Bea a reassuring smile. "As long as we stay away from the abdominal region, we can safely take a few X-rays."

The doctor left, and Freya looked to Bea. "Does Devin know about the baby?"

He had become a part of her life lately, so it made sense Freya would make the correlation. "Yes. We wanted to wait at least another month before telling anyone. Something happened, and we had to tell his ex-wife and his daughter. Otherwise they wouldn't know, either."

As a hospital aid arrived with a wheelchair, a thought popped into Bea's head. She grasped Freya's arm. "Were you able to get ahold of Devin?"

Bea's phone was back at the café. Earlier, before she'd been caught up in the admission process when they'd first arrived at the emergency room, she'd asked her aunt to reach out to him.

"I took care of it." Freya waved her on. "Now you just focus on looking after yourself and my great-niece or nephew."

On the way to get the X-ray, a small bit of anxiety gripped Bea. The fall hadn't hurt the baby, and the doctor hadn't been concerned. But what if she had? This visit to the hospital would have had an entirely different outcome.

Closing her eyes, she wished for Devin. Freya had called him. Undoubtedly, he was on his way. Surprisingly, tears threatened to well up as a sense of relief came over her.

Her climbing stepladders would now be added to the list of things he worried about along with her getting enough sleep and not skipping meals. And right then, she didn't care if Devin gave her a mini lecture when he arrived about taking better care of herself. She just looked forward to the hug and kiss he would give her afterwards.

Once the X-ray was done, she was wheeled back downstairs and taken to a curtained-off patient bay adjacent to the emergency area.

Freya wasn't there. Maybe she was outside meeting Devin?

A moment later, her great-aunt came into the patient bay alone. "There you are. It took two people to tell me where to find you."

"Hopefully Devin, won't have the same problem. I'm surprised he's not here yet."

"Oh, when I called the paper, he wasn't there. I had to convince them to give me his number. He didn't answer his phone, but I left him a message." She patted Bea's arm. "I'm sure he's on his way."

So Freya hadn't actually spoken to him? Had he gotten the message? But even if he hadn't, if he'd stopped by the café, someone would have told him what happened to her. Shouldn't he have already reached out to Freya?

Or had he lost track of time while caught up in a story with his phone off, again? Lauren had said when he was chasing a story, he shut everything out because nothing else mattered.

Bea closed her eyes, trying to erase doubt. But what Lauren and Carly had said about Devin loomed in her mind.

Dr. Hanson came into the patient bay. "Sorry for the delay. But I have good news—you're in the clear. You just have a small bump on the head, no concussion. As far as the ankle, you don't have any joint instability or serious bruising. The pain and swelling should resolve in one to three weeks. Rest, ice, compression, and elevation are all you need. Someone will be in shortly to wrap that ankle for you, and then you're free to go."

"Thank you," Bea said.

A short time later, as they prepared to leave the patient bay, she stood by the bed trying to find her balance with a pair of crutches. Her thoughts about Devin were just as shaky and unsure.

As if reading her mind, Freya gave her an empathetic look. "Should I try to reach Devin again?"

"No."

"Are you sure?" Freya took her phone from her purse. "He's probably worried about you."

"If he was, he would have called—"

The curtain opened, and Devin rushed in. Concern filled his face as he went to Bea. "Are you okay?"

Instead of relief, despair assaulted her. She wasn't okay, and she got the sense nothing would be for a while. But she couldn't just ignore reality.

She sat back down on the bed and propped the crutches beside her. "Freya, would you mind giving us a minute?"

Her aunt gave a quick smile. "I'll be in the waiting room."

After she left, Bea responded to his question. "I'm okay, and so is our baby. Where were you? Freya called the office *and* your phone?"

"Something happened with Carly. My phone rang but I put it on silent to focus on the situation."

"Is she all right?"

"She overheard me and Lauren arguing about the co-parenting agreement and the move." As Devin stood in front of her, he took hold of her hands. "But right now my focus is you.

Until when? First his inattentiveness for the past few days, now this. If something serious had happened that put her or the baby in jeopardy, he wouldn't have been there for her.

Devin cupped her cheek. "Why don't you stay with me for the next few days? I don't have stairs at my place. It will be easier for you to get around, and I can look after you."

Bea swallowed against tightness in her throat. The more she allowed herself to depend on him, the more promises he'd break. And honestly, she just couldn't face the same disappointment with Devin that she'd felt with her ex not being there when she needed him, no matter what the reason. She had to protect her heart. She had to protect *her baby.* He had obligations that didn't include them. And she did love him too much to make him choose. It was best to cut her losses now.

Bea took in a breath, but instead of air coming into her lungs, it felt like a flood of misery. She leaned away from his hand on her cheek. "I can't go home with you, Devin. Trying to turn our co-parenting situation into something else is a mistake."

Devin gripped her hand. "If this is about me not getting here right away, I'm sorry..."

As she glanced down at her still-flat stomach, panic warred with the conviction inside of her. She was scared, but she could do it. Bea met his gaze. "It's just not about that. You have other obligations in your life. But my primary focus is our child. And then the café. I need stability right now to balance everything. And I can't create that if I'm trying to be in a romantic relationship with you. But you're welcome in our baby's life."

Devin looked stricken. "Bea, don't do this."

"No, Devin, please—I've made up my mind." Swallowing hard, she slipped her hand from his. "I'm doing what's best for all of us."

Chapter Twenty-One

Losing Carly, then Bea in the span of twenty-four hours was like a one-two punch, devastating enough to make Devin's head spin and almost knock him to the ground. He hadn't seen it coming.

Devin put a double-espresso pod into the coffeemaker, but he doubted there was enough caffeine in the world to take away the fatigue-laced pain and disbelief clouding his mind.

He'd hoped Carly would want to stay in Chatelaine. Did she want to leave because he was expecting a baby with Bea? But Bea thought he didn't have enough room in his life for her and the baby. Did Carly feel something similar—that she no longer had a place in his life as his daughter?

The questions he pondered late into the night still plagued him. But no clear-cut answers emerged.

Especially when it came to Bea. How had he messed up so badly that she didn't understand how he felt about her? She and the baby were important to him, and he was willing to do anything in his power to make her happy.

His gaze strayed to his phone on the counter, and remorse pinged in his gut for breaking his promise of not ignoring his phone. If only he'd answered Freya's call or checked his messages earlier, he would be taking care of Bea right now instead of missing her.

The phone rang. It was Lauren.

He answered. "Hello."

"Hi." She paused. "How's Bea doing?"

Not wanting to get into it, he gave the simplest answer. "She's fine. What about Carly?" He and Lauren had talked briefly last night after he'd arrived home, but Carly had already gone to bed.

"She hasn't said much to me since last night. And she wasn't like herself when she woke up."

"What do you mean she's not herself?"

"She's fine now. She just seemed really sad. We talked and she's feeling better. I'm taking her to school this afternoon." Hints of concern still hung in Lauren's tone. "But I think she believes you're upset at her."

"Of course I'm not. If moving is what she wants, I accept that." But he couldn't deny the disappointment he felt.

"I know you do," Lauren said. "If it means anything, I was just as surprised as you were to hear that she wanted to move with me to Corpus Christi. She mentioned how excited she was about the baby… I thought she'd want to stay here with you and Bea."

Carly was excited about the baby? He'd missed that, too, along with everything else. "Should I come by?"

"Can you? I think it would help a lot if you talked to her."

"Sure." It didn't matter how dragged down he felt, his daughter needed him. He had to go.

An hour or so later at Lauren's house, Devin walked down the hall to Carly's room. He knocked on the closed door. "Carly. Can I come in?"

"Yes."

He opened the door. "Hey."

His daughter sat cross-legged with her feet tucked under her on the bed. Her attention remained on her phone. "Hi."

He sat on the side of the mattress beside her. "Can we talk?"

"Sure." Carly put her phone aside, but she still wouldn't look at him. She picked at the chipped purple glitter nail polish on her thumb.

"I'm sorry I had to leave before we finished our conversation about you moving to Corpus Christi with your mom. I had to go check on Bea."

"I know. Mom told me." Carly met his gaze. "Is everything okay?"

"Yes. She and the baby are fine."

"I'm glad." She paused. "So you're really not mad at me for not wanting to stay here?"

The trust in her eyes that he'd tell her the truth—he couldn't ignore it. "I'm really not mad about it. But is it hard for me to imagine you not being here? Am I sad that I won't get to see you play volleyball or cheer at a football game? Am I worried about not being there if you need me for something or just want to talk to me. Yes."

"I get it." Excitement and exasperation filled her face. "But hello, Dad, video calls work! We can talk every day, and if I make the volleyball team or the cheerleading squad, Mom can video call you then, too, so you can see me. It would almost be like you were there." She smirked. "And you and everyone else always said Corpus Christi was a straight shot from here. You can come there, or

Mom can drive me here. And in a couple of years, when I'm sixteen, you can buy me a car and I can drive myself."

Drive? It was terrifying just imagining her driving, period. And he and Lauren would never let her travel between Chatelaine and Corpus Christi by herself.

But someday she would turn seventeen and then eighteen and beyond. Driving alone, going off to college, falling in love—it was all in her future. Pride, fear, and love gripped his chest. He wasn't ready for any of it.

"It'll be good, Dad." Carly reached out and took hold of his hand on the mattress.

For a fleeting moment, the vision of her holding on to his hand as she'd been learning to walk flashed in his mind. Back then, she'd grasped onto him with such certainty, knowing she was safe and he wouldn't let her go. He felt that same certainty in her now.

He angled his body more toward his little girl. "So, you really are looking forward to moving?"

"Yes." Her face lit up even more. "Corpus Christi is a city with more things to do. It will be fun. All my friends are jealous."

"So Bea and the baby have nothing to do with you wanting to leave?"

Carly shrugged. "Maybe a little. The baby's going to need you more than I do. And you'll need time to be a great dad for them like you are for me."

The earnestness in her eyes made a lump form in his throat. "Okay, then I guess it's settled."

"Good." She wrapped her arms around his neck and hugged him tight. "And since you're worried about not being there, maybe Francis could come live with me."

Devin chuckled as he hugged her tighter. She had all the answers, didn't she? "We'll see."

A short time later, Devin joined Lauren in the kitchen. Concern was etched on her face. "How did it go?"

"She's good."

"We really messed up by underestimating her, didn't we?" his ex-wife said quietly.

"Yeah, we did. But now we know better."

"We were so concerned about not stressing her out over our disagreement, but that's exactly what we did by not telling her the truth." Lauren huffed a wry chuckle and shook her head. "How did we get it so wrong?"

"I think we forgot we're on the same side. We may not be married anymore, but we want the best for Carly and each other."

"You're right. Let's make a deal not to forget that again. And instead of reacting, we'll focus on really hearing each other's point of view when it comes to Carly."

She held out her hand and Devin shook it. "Deal." Some of the heaviness he'd awakened with that morning lifted. "Before I forget—Carly wants to take Francis with her. It's up to you. I can adopt him, and he can stay here with the two of you before the move. If for some reason it doesn't work out, he can come back and live with me."

As reasonable as it all sounded, he couldn't ignore the pang of sadness echoing inside of him. He'd lost his daughter, the woman he loved, and he was on the verge of losing the dog who'd kept him company for the last few weeks. His life was starting to sound like a sad country song.

Devin dug his keys out of his pocket. "Well, keep me up to date on the details of the move. Let me know what I can do to help."

Lauren studied him. "Something's happened. What's wrong?"

I'm trying to wrap my mind around you taking my daughter. He could use that excuse. But giving her that answer wouldn't be the complete truth. And it would be unfair to lay that on Lauren.

"It's Bea."

"So she's not okay? Oh no—the baby..." From Lauren's expression she anticipated the worse.

Devin hastened to assure her. "They're both fine. It's just that..." Saying it aloud for the first time brought an ache to his chest. "Bea and I aren't together as a couple anymore."

Lauren looked stunned. "I'm sorry." She paused as if unsure of what to say. "Do you want to talk about it? I could make some coffee." Her genuine concern and empathy caught him off guard.

"Sure. I could use some caffeine."

Moments later, he sat on the stool at the kitchen counter with a cup of coffee in front of him.

Lauren stood on the other side of the counter, drinking tea.

The morning she'd told him she was moving to Corpus Christi crossed his mind. So much had occurred since then. Choices. Decisions...and losses.

"So what happened?" she asked.

Devin toyed with the mug on the counter. "Bea said she and the baby needed stability, and because of my devotion to the paper and other responsibilities, she doesn't think I can provide that." Lauren objecting to Carly staying in Chatelaine with him came to mind, and a harsh laugh escaped. "And I guess you probably agree with her."

Lauren took a sip of tea before responding. "You're a

lot of things, but unstable or unreliable isn't one of them. But I can understand why she might feel that way."

He sat back in the chair. "I'm listening."

"Because she doesn't know you like I do. I have years of being married to you and us raising Carly together to back up that knowledge. Bea doesn't have time and certainty to erase her doubts."

"But I'm willing to put in the time," he protested. "I told her from day one that I'm not leaving her to handle the pregnancy or raising our child alone. Shouldn't that count for something?"

"I'm sure it does. But your choices are a big problem."

"I'm choosing her and the baby. How is that a problem?"

Lauren looked directly at him. "You need to choose *yourself*."

He wasn't sure he'd heard her correctly. "You think I should choose myself?"

"Yes." Lauren stalled his forthcoming response with a raised hand. "And before you say that's selfish, listen to me. When your dad got sick, he had to come first. And the paper—it had been one of the top priorities, too, because it was one of the things that kept him going. After that, it was Carly and then our marriage and then you."

"My priorities couldn't have been different. All of you needed me."

"We did, but after your dad passed away, everything on that list changed or moved on, except you…until Bea showed up. She and the pregnancy forced you out of a rut. For the first time in years, you've been anticipating something new in your life, and I have to admit, it's been wonderful to see." She pinned him with a warning look.

"But you'll lose it all if you don't fully embrace the moments that bring you joy—things like spending time with the people you care about and being a great father like your dad was. You've just forgotten how to do it. You've forgotten to be happy."

Devin tried to find something to object to in what Lauren was suggesting, but he couldn't. Those things did matter to him. And he had felt happy with Bea. And looked forward to helping her prepare for their child together.

As he studied Lauren's face something else became clear. Her choices. "The move to Corpus Christi—isn't about money or accepting a promotion. It's about choosing yourself, isn't it?"

"Yes—I had to. My time in Chatelaine is over. It would be easier to stay here and just go with the flow. You were right to stop me yesterday. It would have been a bad decision to turn down the job and stay here. What's best for me is moving ahead and trying something new. And those are the kind of choices Carly needs to see me making—and she needs to see that from you, too."

Later that night, as Devin sat on the back porch reflecting on what Lauren had said, his thoughts drifted to his dad. Carl had been a hard worker, but Devin had always known that his dad had loved him and put him first.

When Carly had come along, his father had often put work aside, thrilled to hold and talk to his granddaughter. The way his dad had truly valued those moments had often made him pause. He could see now that Carl had been reveling in happiness.

Devin's memories shifted to his own moments with Carly. Her first cry as she'd entered the world, the first time she'd stared into his eyes as if she'd known him forever. First words, first steps, first hurts…he'd been there.

The vision in his mind morphed to Bea holding a baby. *Their baby.* And him not being a part of it. And worse, he'd no longer laugh with Bea, hold her, wake up with her, experience life with her. More images of all they'd miss out on together as a couple and a family flashed into his mind. His heart ached. He wanted a chance to build a life and a family with Bea. But would she give him another chance?

Chapter Twenty-Two

Bea trudged to the kitchen in her condo, flipping on lights along the way. It was before dawn, but more sleep wasn't in her future. She couldn't stop thinking about the baby and the future…and Devin.

Almost a week had passed since their breakup, and just as she'd requested, he hadn't contacted her. However, he had reached out to Esme to make sure she was okay.

It was good to have her sister back. Esme had been shocked to hear all that had happened since the wedding. But as expected, she'd been so supportive.

Bea went to the pantry and took out the box of lemon-ginger tea. It was the kind Devin had brewed for her the night she'd met Carly.

Once the hot drink was prepared, she sat down at the kitchen table. As she took a sip, comfort and warmth surrounded her, reminding her of Devin's embrace on the porch swing. She soaked it all in, wishing he were there. Heartache started to tighten its hold, threatening to unloose tears. No. She'd cried bucketloads over the past three days. It was time to stop.

Closing her eyes, she forced herself to breathe. "We'll be okay. Things might be a little bumpy at first, but I promise I'll figure it out."

It took a moment for Bea to realize she wasn't just talking to herself. She rested her hand on her stomach. Could the baby hear and sense what she was feeling? If so, she really *did* have to pull herself together, and go back to work. She'd been resting her ankle, and it did feel better. It was time to start adjusting to her new normal—being a single, pregnant business owner on her way to becoming a single mom. She also needed to really tackle the newborn-essentials checklist.

At some point, she should probably contact Devin about some of the things on the list. But designing and setting up the nursery was on her.

As the sun started to light up the sky, the doorbell rang. Who was stopping by this early? She checked the doorbell video camera.

It was Freya and Esme.

Bea answered the door, and as they walked in, each of the women gave her a hug.

Esme studied Bea's face before meeting her gaze. "You're not sleeping. Is it nausea or something else?"

Bea read between the lines about what "something else" meant. "No, I'm feeling okay." She and Esme looped arms as they followed Freya into the kitchen. "I just really miss my caffeine boosts in the morning. But coffee just doesn't taste the same."

"Cutting back on caffeine is probably a good thing." Her aunt dropped her purse onto one of the chairs at the kitchen table. "But food is important. When was the last time you ate?"

"Umm—yesterday." Freya's and Esme's pointed looks prompted Bea to confess. "Yesterday afternoon. I had some soup, but it was really filling."

"Soup?" Freya shook her head in disapproval. "No, you need a good meal." She went to the pantry. "Regular oatmeal. That's a start."

Esme perused the shelves in the refrigerator. "And there's fruit. I'll cut some up. And if you don't mind, I'll take some oatmeal, too."

Bea got up to help, but Esme nudged her back to the table. "Sit. We got this."

A short time later, oatmeal, sliced apples, and toast with peach jam sat in front of Bea at the table.

Esme and Freya joined her for breakfast.

As Bea took a bite of toast with jam, her tastebuds perked up, and suddenly she was ravenous for more jam.

The memory of feeding Devin peach tartlets with whipped cream hit her at the same time that she sucked jam from her fingertips. Tears welled then spilled from her eyes.

"Oh, honey." Esme slid her chair closer and wrapped her arm around Bea's shoulders. "What is it?"

"Peaches…" Bea swallowed the words. "This is insane. What's wrong with me?"

"Pregnancy hormones." Freya patted Bea's hand.

Bea dried her cheeks with the napkin Esme handed her. "Am I going to do this every time I think about him?"

"Probably." Freya released a breezy chuckle. "The only way to make you feel better about it would be to have him here."

"No. We can't be together. It won't work." Bea looked to Esme for backup, but her sister wouldn't meet her gaze. "You agree with Aunt Freya?"

Esme offered up a delicate shrug. "From what you've told me and what else I've heard, you *were* happy with Devin."

"I was, but it's not just about me. As much as I care about him, I have to put our baby first. And part of that is not setting Devin up for failure by expecting him to be there. I know what it's like to be let down. I went through it with Jeff."

Her sister frowned. "You're comparing Devin to your ex? Is that fair? You said Devin *had* been there since the moment he found out you were pregnant."

"He was—as best he could. And I know he wants to do the right thing now, but…" Bea searched for the words to explain. "The newspaper is important to him. His daughter is important to him. I don't want to make him choose."

"Making choices are about learning to find balance. That's something you'll have to learn, too. And it doesn't happen overnight," Esme reminded her. "Ryder and I are still figuring it all out when it comes to us and the boys and our jobs. The one thing I do know is that finding the right balance as a couple takes practice and learning things along the way." She gently nudged Bea with her shoulder. "And allowing for mistakes. They happen. No one's perfect, especially as a parent."

"She's right," Freya said. "And relationships in general take a lot of work, and learning how to make things work takes time. And that's where love comes in." A nostalgic, faraway expression briefly came over her face. She focused back on Bea. "I saw you and Devin together. What you felt for each other was evident. You two were in love. And love makes all things possible."

The doorbell rang.

"I'll get it." Esme went to answer the door. A moment later, she came back with a cardboard box imprinted with a pink-and-blue design. Grinning, she handed it to Bea. "You've got a special delivery."

Bea studied the package. "Who's it from?"

Esme clapped her hands in encouragement. "Open it and find out."

Bea unsealed the box. Arranged in the colorful packing were an assortment of items: lotions and other pampering products and candles with a heavenly soothing scent.

She opened the envelope attached to the lid and read the card inside of it. "'Welcome to Well Mama Sunshine. Each month, you'll receive a box with curated items for moms-to-be.'" Happiness sparked a smile. "Did you two do this?"

Freya and Esme looked to each other, then shook their heads.

"But it's adorable," Esme said. "Oh, look. There's a stack of laminated cards with the votives. I think they're affirmations." She picked one of them up and smiled.

"What does it say?" Bea asked.

"Exactly what you needed to hear."

Bea accepted the card from her sister and read it.

I am loved.

Over the next few days, more surprises from an anonymous source showed up: a spa bundle including monthly massages, an appointment with a personal stylist at a maternity store plus a generous clothing allowance, and a paid subscription to a grocery and personal-item delivery service.

Sitting at her desk at the restaurant, Bea finished the signup process for the latter. The subscription was a thoughtful gesture, just like the rest of the gifts. Despite eating many of her meals at the café, she still needed to stock her own refrigerator.

But who was sending her the gifts? She'd quizzed family and friends. It was easy to imagine them getting together to arrange this, especially to show their support and cheer her up after injuring her ankle. But they all denied involvement.

Was it Devin? Should she reach out to him to see if he was sending the gifts?

Her heart leaped at the possibility of him as the anonymous gift giver, but then she tamped down excitement. What if she was wrong? What if he *was* respecting her wishes and staying away from her? Acceptance mixed with regret and sadness pinged inside of Bea.

She missed him so much. And it had become impossible not to think about him. One of the things that brought her comfort was the candles in the gift box. Their scent was so soothing, she couldn't resist lighting one the past few nights when she'd arrived home from work. And it was uplifting to read the affirmation cards at the start of her day. The message from the one she'd picked that morning had continued to stick with her.

By doing the best for my well-being, I am doing the best for my baby.

Since her talk with Esme and Freya, she'd debated what the best thing was when it came to her and Devin. They were right—Devin wasn't her ex-husband. And he probably was overscheduled. And she was in love with him. But what if love wasn't enough? If things didn't work out with Devin. She'd feel like...*a failure.*

Bea sank back heavily into the chair. Okay, she could admit it now. It wasn't so much about setting up Devin for failure. She didn't want to set up *herself* for failure. Her marriage ending with Jeff had hurt, but looking back now, she could see the commitment they'd shared had been a shallow imitation of a relationship. What she'd shared with Devin had been real. If they were together and it didn't work out…it would hurt much more.

A knock sounded at her open door.

A dark-haired, middle-aged man in a Western-style shirt and jeans peeked in. "Hello, Ms. Fortune. The person out front directed me to your office. I'm Milt—from Milt Handyman Services." He strode in and gave her a business card. "I was passing through this afternoon and just wanted to introduce myself in person. I was also hoping we could work out a time for us to discuss your project."

"Yes. Come in." Bea mentally went through her schedule. Esme had probably set up something with him and forgotten to tell her. "Which project are you referring to—is it something in the kitchen or the dining room?"

Milt looked puzzled. "I don't know anything about a kitchen or a dining room. I'm renovating a room that will be used as a baby nursery. I have the specs here." He took his phone from his pocket and tapped the screen. "Sea-green walls and ceiling. White trim. Bench seat for a window, and…"

"And a pocket door leading to the bathroom."

"Exactly." He grinned. "Whew. For a minute there, I thought I was talking to the wrong person. So mainly I just need…"

As Milt talked, Bea filled in the blanks. Only one person would know all of the details he'd described. Devin. She'd sent him the link to her dream nursery…and now he was making it a reality.

She wrestled with the surprise and happiness swelling inside of her. Was this his way of making amends for the mistakes he'd made? Was it enough? On some level, this wonderful, thoughtful action felt too big to ignore. It felt like an opening. A chance. A sign that what she and Devin shared could actually work.

Maybe this backed up Freya's claim that love made all things possible.

As Bea sorted through her thoughts, a question surfaced. The affirmation card she'd pulled that morning had stated she was doing the best for herself. But by not allowing for mistakes or another chance to make a relationship work, *was* she doing the best thing when it came to her and Devin and their child?

Chapter Twenty-Three

Devin sat at the head of the table during the late-morning meeting in the conference room. It was strange but also good to have another key staff member there besides just him, Quinn, and Charles.

Adele, the new assistant editor, had started three days ago and was already fitting in well with the team.

Having her there was especially helpful since Devin's mind was occupied with other tasks outside of the day-to-day with the paper. Absently, he grazed his thumb over a rough spot on his palm. A splinter—he thought he'd removed it last night, but part of it was still there. As aggravating as the damn thing was, the small discomfort was a happy reminder of the projects he was working on in the room adjoining his office and at his house. And strangely he had Lauren to thank for it.

He was also planning to tackle the newborn-essentials list and the questionnaire item by item, but first he was looking after Bea's well-being...anonymously.

In a week or so, he would reach out to her directly. Maybe by then, she would be open to seeing him, and he could show her what he'd been working on for the baby. They were just a few of the changes he was making—along with hiring more people to free up his schedule. He missed her so much and would give anything to be with her again or hear her voice. But he would give her what she'd asked of him. Time.

"I really think we need to move the article about the upcoming town council meeting to the front page," Adele said. The dark-haired Latina in her mid-thirties, studied her tablet with the draft of the upcoming newspaper on the screen. "Land zoning is current news. A lot of people are interested in what's going to happen with the upcoming proposal."

Charles nodded. "I agree, especially since it isn't just a hot topic here but in the surrounding towns, too. In fact, we might consider a series of articles on this. It would also be a good way for our new reporter at large to get acquainted with the area."

The other new hire joining the team in a week was relocating from San Antonio to Chatelaine.

All eyes turned to Devin. "Sounds good. Let's move the article to the front page. And as far as the series, write up a proposal with the angles for each of the articles, and we'll discuss it."

A chime sounded from the door in the reception area.

As Quinn went to see who it was, the group continued to discuss other changes.

A moment later, she returned. "Devin—Bea's here. She's waiting in your office."

"She is?" He immediately rose to his feet. Just as he reached the door, Devin remembered they were in the midst of a meeting. "Let's take a fifteen-minute break. But if I'm not back by then, keep going without me."

He strode to his office a couple of doors down. As soon

as he saw Bea sitting on the couch, his heart thumped an extra beat in his chest.

"Hello." As Bea stood, a hint of anxiety reflected in her eyes. Just like that day in the parking lot when she'd told him she was pregnant.

Awkwardness and uncertainty. That wasn't what he wanted for their future.

Tamping down his own anxiety, he smiled back. "Hi."

As he shut the door behind him, Bea came closer. "You're working on the next edition of the paper—I'm sorry. I should have called. I won't take up too much of your time."

"No. You're fine." He couldn't stop his gaze from straying to the door leading to the other room. *Whew.* Good thing he'd closed it before going to the meeting earlier that morning.

"But aren't you on a deadline?"

"We are, but my staff can handle it."

They really didn't need him. The realization of that really hit Devin. For once, he didn't feel stressed out, trying to beat the clock. Hell, he could take the entire afternoon off. If he would have been able to do that weeks ago, maybe he and Bea wouldn't have broken up.

Regret needled him as he approached her. It was difficult not to reach out and touch her. "How are you?"

"I'm good. Really good. And so is the baby." Her genuine smile brought a glow to her face.

Words he couldn't stop just came out. "You look beautiful."

"Thank you." A light flush came into her cheeks enhancing her natural radiance. "I…well, like I said, I feel good." She glanced down as if gathering her thoughts. "A handyman stopped by my office earlier this morning.

He said someone hired him to turn the guest room at my condo into a nursery."

"Really?" He injected surprise into his tone. "I wonder who set that up?"

From Bea's raised brow she already knew the answer.

Devin softly chuckled. "I guess I need to work on my poker face."

"Just a little. Actually, the handyman gave you away. He showed me the plans only you would know about." She stepped closer. "You didn't have to hire him. I don't expect you to renovate my home."

"I know..." Unable to stop himself, Devin reached out and took her hand. Pain shot into his from the splinter, and he immediately let go. He shook off the discomfort.

Bea frowned in concern. "What's wrong?"

"It's nothing. I just have a splinter in my palm."

She took his hand in hers. The sting faded as she gently caressed the red spot on his skin.

"You need to take this out."

The softness and concern in her gaze along with her scent were too alluring to ignore. Devin swallowed hard. "I will when I get home later tonight."

"Tonight?" Bea released him, and he immediately missed her touch. "No, this could get infected. Hold on." She went to her purse sitting on the couch and dug through it. A few seconds later, she pulled tweezers from a small cosmetic bag. "Let me see."

He walked over to her.

Bea firmly grasped his hand, inspecting the reddened spot. "The end of it is sticking out. I think I can get it." She probed his palm with the tweezers. "Sorry. I know this hurts."

"I'm good." The ache in his chest at the thought of losing her was far worse than his hand. He'd endure the pain a hundred times over if he could hold and kiss Bea again.

"Almost..." She held up the splinter with a triumphant expression. "I got it."

"Thank you. I'm lucky you were carrying around a pair of tweezers." On a reflex his hand tightened around hers.

Bea didn't pull away. "They came in the pregnancy pampering box I received the other day." She glanced down a moment. "If you're doing these things as an apology or because you feel guilty, please don't. It isn't necessary. I don't hate you or anything close to that."

Guilt? He hadn't realized Bea might see it that way. "No. That's not what this is about. Come with me. I need to show you something."

Devin led Bea to the side door to the adjoining room. Nervousness assaulted him as he gripped the knob. It wasn't finished yet, but hopefully she'd approve of what he'd done so far.

Holding his breath, he opened the door.

Bea gasped. "Oh, Devin..."

Glancing around the room with new beige carpeting and sea-green painted walls, he tried to imagine it through her eyes. He walked to the boxes stacked in the corner. "I bought three of the cribs you wanted—one for here, for the nursery at your condo once it's done, and the one I'm setting up at my house.

"The rocking recliner is from a store in Corpus Christi. It's really comfortable. I chose the leather one, but they have different upholstery options if you want one of those, too."

Devin turned to the wood cabinet connected to the wall.

"I'm building another one of these with a changing table plus counter space for things like a bottle warmer. And the open space over here—that's where I'm putting the mini refrigerator. I'm almost done with the one at my house." As he saw the rooms completed in his mind, he smiled.

It faded as he spotted Bea, staring at the room with a shocked, weepy expression. Did he make a mistake or get something wrong?

He hurried over to her. "If you don't like what I've done—"

"No." She shook her head. "I love it. But when did you have time to do all of this?"

"I've made some changes. I hired two new staff members to lighten the load. And I'll bring in more people if I have to." As Devin faced her, he lightly grasped her shoulders. "Guilt or trying to make an apology has nothing to do with this. I want to help take care of our child. We both work, and at times, we'll have to use a sitter. But I can watch over them here, too, and you can come by during the day whenever you're free."

Visions filled his mind as he glanced around the room. "I'm looking forward to sitting over there and feeding our child. Or rocking him or her to sleep." He chuckled. "I'm even looking forward to changing diapers. I want a chance to embrace more of their precious milestones instead of missing them."

He took her hands in his and grabbed hold of possibility. "The one thing that would make it all complete would be a second chance with you. I know I disappointed you. And I understand—"

Bea pressed her lips to his, cutting off his words.

Devin slipped his arms around her. The yearning he'd

kept in check for far too long short-circuited his thoughts, and he held her close, losing himself in the lush warmth of her mouth and her soft curves pressed against him.

But as much as he wanted to keep kissing her, he couldn't hold back on what else he needed to say.

Devin held on to her waist and eased out of the kiss. "You said you don't hate me, and I'm really glad about that. I'm sorry for not simplifying my life sooner—if I had, it would have prevented a lot of stress between us. The last thing I ever wanted was for you to doubt whether or not you could count on me."

Bea laid her hand on his chest. "You can't take all the blame. I added stress to our relationship, too. I gave in to focusing on my past experiences instead of what was standing right in front of me. You."

"I'm glad to hear that." Breathing away anxiety, he dived back in. "But there's something else you should know. I'm falling in love with you—and not just because we're having a baby together. It started the moment we danced at the reception."

"That's good to know." She met his gaze. "Because that's when I started falling in love with you."

Happiness fueled Devin's smile. Leaning away, he glanced down at her stomach. "Did you hear that? Your mama's falling in love with me."

Bea laughed. "If my growling stomach is the answer, they heard you."

"Then we should eat. Where do you want to go?"

"What about your place or mine? We can talk things through...and see where it leads."

The look of desire in her eyes made his heart leap. He

brought her closer. "Should I clear my calendar for the rest of the day?"

Bea leaned more against him. "That's what I planned to do."

"I like that plan…a lot." Devin kissed her, grateful for a second chance at love and a bigger life.

Epilogue

Five Months Later

Bea woke up to her back being spooned against Devin's front. As he stretched his strong arm around her, he curved his hand over the swell of her baby bump, enveloping her in a hug.

He brushed a kiss along her temple. "Good morning."

A contented sigh escaped from her. "Good morning." As she pushed back against him, instead of his bare legs and chest, she encountered clothing. "Why are you dressed?"

"I'm going downstairs to make breakfast with Carly. Do you need anything?"

Bea turned in his arms. As he rolled to his back, she rested her head on his chest. He wore a T-shirt and sweatpants. The softness of the fabric, his warmth, and the light, appealing fragrance of the aftershave lotion he used prompted her to snuggle against him. "Just you."

"Too easy, sweetheart. You've already got me."

His soft kiss to her forehead and the slight tightening of his arms around her suddenly made her want to cry with happiness and pee at the same time. Bea managed to hold back the water works on both ends, wanting another minute or two in his arms.

She'd never felt so cherished and cared for in her life as she had these past few months with Devin. He'd kept his word about cutting back on his schedule, especially on weekends. She looked forward to spending these early morning hours together.

"Do you want anything special for breakfast?" he asked. "We still have fresh peaches left over from yesterday. I can make pancakes with peaches and cinnamon again."

As much as Bea loved snuggling with him, hunger for food suddenly moved to the top of her list of needs. Her mouth watered. Pancakes sounded great but… "Is a breakfast pizza too much to ask for?"

He chuckled. "Not at all. Carly guessed that was probably what you'd want. She already made the dough. Eggs, cheese, and turkey bacon okay?

"Perfect."

Devin gave her a quick kiss, then went to the kitchen.

After taking care of the essentials in the bathroom, Bea headed downstairs.

Devin and Carly were talking.

"What about Baxter or a cool name like Hipparanamus?" he said with humor in his tone. "We could call him Bax or Harry for short."

Carly laughed. "Seriously, Dad? Those aren't close to cool names for my baby brother. What about Nick or Jaeden? Or Francis?"

The mixed terrier, who was now a permanent part of the family, barked as if he understood.

Baby brother… It was so good to hear Carly make that claim. Day by day they were growing closer, especially since she'd been spending the summer with them and was working at the Cowgirl Café.

Over the past few months, the restaurant had become popular not only in Chatelaine but also the surrounding area. So many good things were happening in their lives. Sometimes it felt like a dream, but it wasn't. This was her life now and Bea was grateful for all of it.

As she walked into the kitchen, Devin and Carly both looked up from where they were adding toppings to pizza dough in a pan on the counter.

Grinning, he pointed to the small, black dry-erase board on the front of the refrigerator. "You're just in time to give an opinion on the latest baby names to add to the list."

"I heard."

"So are you on board with Hipparanamus?" He wiggled his brows playfully."

"Yeah…no. I think I'm with Carly and Francis on this round. And I have another one to add."

As Bea made her way to the refrigerator, Francis followed. His tail thumped on the ground as he sat beside her.

"Hey, cutie." She gave him a head rub before sliding the marker from the holder on the door and adding *Nick* and *Jaeden* to the list plus one more.

Carly went to Bea. The teen smiled as she saw what Bea had written. "I actually kind of like it."

"I…" A small fluttering like butterfly wings spread just below Bea's belly button, and she released a surprised gasp.

"Are you okay?" Carly asked.

"Yes, I'm fine. It's the baby." Laughing, she took Carly's hand and placed it where she'd felt the baby kick. "I think he likes the name, too."

"I feel him." Awe and excitement filled Carly's expression. "Dad, come here—you have to feel this."

"On my way." Devin quickly put the pizza into the oven.

Carly glanced down at the dog who was fidgeting around them. "It's time for his potty break. Come on, Francis." She ushered the dog out the kitchen.

Devin reached Bea. He did a double take at what she'd written on the board. Smiling, he embraced her from behind. "Are you sure?"

The baby kicked again.

As Bea looked over her shoulder and met his gaze, her heart swelled with happiness and the same love she saw in his eyes. "I think it's decided. In a few more months, Devin Street Jr. will make his appearance."

Devin smiled. "I can't wait to meet him."

She turned in his arms to face him. "Neither can I." Bea met Devin for a kiss, excited for the future ahead of them…as a family.

* * * * *

West Fortune is back from the dead!
Don't miss

Fortune's Lonestar Twins
By Teri Wilson

Available May 2024 wherever
Harlequin books and ebooks are sold!

And until then, catch up with the
whole Chatelaine Fortunes clan:

Fortune's Baby Claim
By Michelle Major

Fortune in Name Only
By Tara Taylor Quinn

Available now!